DINNY AND DREAMDUST

DINNY AND DREAMDUST

by Doris Townsend

Illustrated by Sam Savitt

A SIGNAL BOOK
Doubleday & Company, Inc.
Garden City, New York

Other Signal Books

Library of Congress Catalog Card Number 62-11293
Copyright © 1962 by Doubleday & Company, Inc.
All Rights Reserved
Printed in the United States of America

Prepared by ℞ Rutledge Books
First Edition

CONTENTS

DINNY AND DREAMDUST

CHAPTER 1

Trouble at the Lazy H

Dinny Stoner took the porch steps two at a time, let herself in and slammed the door behind her. Then she stopped and opened the door again. "Be a lady," she told herself. "It really doesn't hurt a bit." This time she closed it gently.

How quiet the house was! But she was used to that. In the three years since her mother died she had learned not to let the silence bother her. Dinny was sixteen now, and much more grown up than the little thirteen-year-old girl who had been so lonely without her mother. All the same, Dinny thought with a sigh, it would be awfully nice to come home to find someone waiting.

Then her face lighted up as she remembered that this morning she would not be alone for long. She and her friend Lissa Lambert had a date to go horseback riding. Any minute now, Lissa would be coming to pick her up.

As if answering her thought, there was a knock on the door.

"You're late!" Dinny said as she flung the door open.

Lissa, blonde with gray eyes, looked at her calmly. "Now suppose I had turned out to be a stranger? You didn't even take time to see who was at the door. Wouldn't you have felt pretty silly telling some complete stranger he was late? Anyway, you just got here yourself. I saw you running into the house as I turned the corner."

In spite of the fact that Lissa was almost a head taller, Dinny always felt a little clumsy in her presence, as if she had suddenly sprouted an extra set of arms and legs.

"But I have already been downtown and back," Dinny explained. "I will bet you didn't get up more than fifteen minutes ago. Come on in, Lissa. I will be ready in a minute."

The difference between the two girls had never been more marked than it was this morning. Dressed in tan riding pants, well-polished boots and a light linen jacket, Lissa looked like a fashion model. Cool and graceful, she always seemed to be the master of any situation.

Dinny, on the other hand, was forever in a hurry, flying through the days as if they did not have nearly enough hours to suit her. She was small and slim and her quick, sweet smile, her amber eyes, her short hair the color of dark butter-scotch added up to more in the way of good looks than she gave herself credit for. The only thing the two girls had in common was their love for riding.

Lissa smiled slowly as she followed Dinny into the house. "I have been up for half an hour. What's your hurry, Dinny? The horses will wait. Now if it were boys we had a date with, I might push myself a little more."

"Boys!" Dinny said with scorn. "Give me horses any day. Horses are reliable!"

That remark stirred Lissa to action. She turned to face Dinny, her eyes wide.

"Honestly, Diane Stoner! Any girl who is not interested in boys just is not—is not *human,* that's all. Why—" Then, seeing the look on Dinny's face, she stopped. "Oh, you are only teasing. You *are* only teasing, aren't you?"

"I am only teasing," Dinny assured her. "Don't get all upset. Just the same, boys are not as important as you think they are." She grinned. "Nothing is *that* important."

"You are only saying that," Lissa said, "because you don't date much yourself. Your father won't let you."

Dinny's face clouded. "I don't mind. Since Dad lost Mom he seems to figure he has to be extra careful about me. But fathers just don't understand that daughters do grow up. I guess fathers don't understand daughters, period. Not the way mothers do. After all, what father was ever a daughter himself, I ask you?"

Dinny gave her head a little shake and changed the

11

subject. "Sit down and wait a second, will you, Lissa? I have to go up to my room for a minute."

"What are you going to wear?" Lissa wanted to know. To Lissa, clothes were next in importance to boys.

Laughing, Dinny looked down at her old boots, her faded jeans, her shirt with its tail out.

"Wear? What I have on, of course. Believe me, Lissa, horses are not impressed by riding habits, and out at the Lazy H Ranch there is no one else to impress. Be right back!"

In her room, Dinny took a small blue book out of the pocket of her shirt and slipped it under a pile of handkerchiefs in the top drawer of her dresser. It was her bank book, and it now showed—with this morning's ten-dollar deposit—a total of one hundred dollars.

It had taken Dinny over a year to save this money. Her "Dreamdust Fund" she called it, because Dreamdust was the name of the beautiful horse Dinny wanted to buy.

Ever since she had learned to ride more than four years ago, Dinny had wanted Dreamdust for her own more than she had ever wanted anything. She and the mare had been riding partners all that time. You could almost say that they were the best of friends. They just had to be together.

Dinny closed the dresser drawer and left the room. As she started down the stairs, she felt lonely again, in spite of the fact that Lissa was waiting for her.

"What's wrong, Dinny?" Lissa asked when she saw the frown on Dinny's face. "You look as if you have just lost your best friend."

"Oh, Lissa, there is a chance I might never see Dreamdust again after today. Dad told me he had heard the Lazy H might be sold. And that would mean the horses would be sold, too. I just can't bear to think about it."

"Dinny, that's a shame. I hope it isn't true." Lissa's eyes, meeting Dinny's troubled ones, were full of sympathy. Maybe she did not agree with Dinny about a lot of things, but she could easily understand how her friend must feel about the little mare.

"So that is why you were so determined to have me go riding at Lazy H with you this morning," Lissa said as the two girls left the house and started toward the bus stop. "You were afraid if I didn't see the Lazy H—and Dreamdust, of course—today, I might never get another chance?" She was silent a moment.

"Hey, how about your bank account? Wasn't that supposed to be for Dreamdust? What happened?"

"Oh, I still have the money. But Mr. Baron—he is the manager of the stable—says that Dreamdust is worth at least two hundred dollars. I have only half that much . . ."

"Maybe," Lissa said, "the people who buy the stable will keep it the way it is now. Then you can go on riding Dreamdust and saving up to buy her." She caught Dinny's arm. "Look! There's our bus—come on!"

Half an hour later the two girls got off the bus at a country road and began to walk the short distance to the stable. At the top of a hill they paused and Dinny exclaimed, "There it is!"

Lissa caught her breath, delighted by what she saw. "I have never ridden anywhere but at Cottonwood Hills," she said softly, "and this is nothing like Cottonwood. But—it is really beautiful!"

Below, to the girls' left, was a big white house with a porch around three sides. Just behind the house was a barn, painted red as all good barns should be. Running out at right angles to the barn was the narrow stall house. Here the horses were kept. At the end of the stall house was the tack room, where the saddles and blankets and other equipment were stored. A waist-high rail fence ran from the tack room door back to the barn, to close the square. At this fence saddled horses, waiting for riders, were usually tied.

Dinny caught Lissa's hand. "Come on—let's hurry! Once I get to this spot, I just can't wait!"

Mr. Baron, the manager, was nowhere in sight when the girls reached the ranch. For this, Dinny was grateful. The less she had to do with him the better. As they entered the stable, Dreamdust greeted Dinny with a happy neigh. For a moment or two Dinny stood with her arm around the little mare's neck, scratching the tickle-spots behind her ears. Lissa rubbed the horse's soft nose.

"She is just beautiful," Lissa said. "No wonder you want to own her."

Dinny chose a gray horse for Lissa. "Can you saddle him, or shall I do it?"

"Don't worry," Lissa told her. "There may be a lot of grooms and stable boys to wait on you at Cottonwood Hills, but we are taught to saddle up all the same."

With Dinny in the lead, the girls went for a long ride in the hills. They stayed out past the usual hour, although Dinny knew Mr. Baron would charge for every minute. "What does it matter?" she thought. "If there is no reason for a Dreamdust Fund any more, what is the use of saving?"

When they got back, Mr. Baron was forking straw into the stalls in the stable. He gave Dinny an ugly look when she introduced Lissa.

"How long you been out?" he demanded, without even looking at Lissa. Mr. Baron knew from experience that Dinny would not shave one second off, so he never bothered to time her.

Glancing at the stable clock, Dinny told him, "An hour and thirty-five minutes," and began to take the saddle off Dreamdust.

After a moment, remembering that this was a do-it-yourself kind of stable and there were no stable boys to help as there were at Cottonwood, Lissa did the same for the gray horse. While the girls were taking the saddles and blankets to the tack room to put on wooden racks to dry, the horses found their way back to their own stalls at opposite ends of the stable.

After she had taken care of the saddles and blankets, Dinny entered Dreamdust's stall and began to rub down the mare's shiny coat with a stiff brush.

Taking another brush, Lissa went to the far end of the stall house and began rubbing down the gray horse.

Just then Mr. Baron came along the runway, the wooden board passage between the stalls. He stopped to watch Dinny.

"He hasn't shaved for a week, or taken a bath, either," Dinny thought. "Better to look at Dreamdust, who is a whole lot prettier. And neater, too, if you get right down to it!"

"Come out for one last ride, I see." The stable manager grinned as he watched Dinny to see what effect the remark would have.

Dinny's heart turned over. "Wh-what did you say?"

"You heard me. Last ride, I said."

"You mean . . ." The words caught in Dinny's throat. She had to swallow hard and begin over again. "You mean the Lazy H has really been sold?"

Mr. Baron shook his head. "No. Seems that the old guy who owned the place willed it to some nephew of his. Well, this nephew has decided to move in and run the place himself. Big fool, if you ask me. Ought to sell and take the money."

He looked around him with disgust. "Nurse maid to a bunch of horses—what a business for a man to be in!" He rammed his elbow into Dreamdust's side and laughed when the mare protested with a loud neigh.

"The horses don't like you any better than you like them," Dinny thought. But she knew better than to say it out loud. She had learned long ago that if you annoyed Mr. Baron he took his anger out on the animals. They could not talk back, and he was careful to stay clear of their hoofs and teeth.

Mr. Baron stumped off to the other end of the stable, leaving Dinny to think over what he said. "But thinking,"

Dinny told herself, "will not help." Nothing would help. Nothing she could do, at least. Or—wait a minute! Maybe there *was* something. Slipping past the little mare, Dinny rushed down the runway toward the stable manager.

"Mr. Baron, I have a hundred dollars saved up. Couldn't you sell me Dreamdust for that?" She waited, holding her breath. Since she got no answer, she went on. "Or—or perhaps I could make it a hundred and fifty. My father might lend me the extra money."

There was a gleam in the old man's eye, but only for a moment. He shook his head. "No. Couldn't see my way clear. Mare is worth two hundred. More, matter of fact. Anyway, I couldn't sell now at any price. 'Just leave everything as it is till the new owner gets here,' the lawyer fellow told me, and that's what I aim to do. Now you clear out and let me get ahead with my work."

Dinny knew it was no use trying to talk to him. She went back to grooming Dreamdust while her mind ran round and round like a trapped animal, searching for a solution to her problem.

After a few minutes Lissa slipped into the stall beside her. "What an awful old man!" she whispered. "Listen, whoever the new owner is, he is sure to be better than Mr. Baron! For all you know, he might turn the Lazy H into a successful riding stable again!"

Before Dinny could answer, Mr. Baron came down the runway with a pail full of water in each hand. "Might be you can strike up a deal with this new owner," he said. "Might be your little offer will look pretty good to this Macklin guy who is taking over."

"Well, I will certainly try," Dinny began. Then she stopped short. "Did you say the new owner is named Macklin? Did he ever live here? We used to know—"

"Search me. Never laid eyes on the poor sucker in my life." As Mr. Baron started to move on he stumbled over a loose board, spilling water from one of the pails into Dreamdust's stall.

"Watch out!" Lissa cried.

"Be careful—you know wet straw gives horses sore feet!" Dinny protested. Quickly the two girls began to kick the wet straw away.

"So what? Quit that!" Mr. Baron ordered in an angry voice. "Mess up my nice, clean stable, will you?"

Dinny thought of several things to say, but she kept them to herself, knowing that if she made the old man more angry, Dreamdust would suffer for it. Lissa was not as wise. "Clean?" she mocked. "Your nice *clean* stable?"

Mr. Baron set down the pails. "A horse is just a horse—couldn't matter less!"

He glared at the girls as if he dared them to answer back. When they did not, he lifted his foot slowly and kicked over one of the pails, sending a small river into Dreamdust's stall. Then, with an ugly smile on his face, he stamped off.

"Don't say anything," Dinny whispered to Lissa. "It will only make things worse. Just—just let's get out of here before I do something crazy, like throwing the other pail of water at him!"

Dinny swept the water out of Dreamdust's stall. Then, throwing an arm around the mare's neck, she said goodby, and rushed from the stable.

But Mr. Baron was not quite finished. "Ranch will be closed next three weeks," he shouted at Dinny. "Might be once this Macklin gets a look at the place, he will throw up his hands and close for good. Might be this is the last time you will ever see your precious Dreamdust!"

Realizing that she could not answer without showing her hurt, Dinny kept going, chin up and shoulders squared.

Lissa ran along beside her until they were out of sight of the Lazy H. Then Dinny leaned against the trunk of a tree and let the tears come.

"Don't!" Lissa urged. "Dinny, don't cry. You shouldn't let that horrible old man make you so mad."

Dinny nodded. "I know. I would like to—to—oh, I don't know what I wouldn't like to do to him! That's the trouble with me and my temper. It's so bad sometimes I am scared of what I will do if I let go of it. And sometimes I just cannot hold it in, either." She gave Lissa a tiny smile through the tears.

"It is not very nice to admit," Dinny went on, "but I

keep my temper best where horses are concerned. With Mr. Baron, for instance, I control my anger because I know if I don't he takes it out on the horses. When it is people who might get hurt, sometimes I am not that smart!"

"You won't have to worry about Mr. Baron any more," Lissa reminded her. "He will be gone. And for all you know, this Mr. Macklin will run the stable the way it ought to be run. Maybe—didn't you say you used to know a Mr. Macklin?"

Dinny nodded. "He was an old friend of Daddy's."

"Well, then, can't you look on the bright side? Can't you hope this is the *right* Mr. Macklin?"

"Yes." Dinny sighed. "But—oh, Lissa, I just can't let myself hope too hard. It seems that every time I want something very much it turns out the exact opposite! Sometimes it's me—I spoil things for myself, I mean. But this time there is not one thing I can do about it, right or wrong. I will just have to wait and see—and that is about as hard to do as anything I know!"

CHAPTER 2

Dreamdust's New Owners

Three weeks later, Dinny Stoner got off the bus and began to walk toward the Lazy H.

"What a difference," she thought, "between today and the last time I was here!"

Dinny was bursting with happiness. The notice in the mail said that the Lazy H was going to open for business again. Better than that, across the bottom of the printed notice was a note that read, "I am just dying to see you again—Janet." That meant that all of Dinny's hopes were realized. Yes, the Macklins who had been left the Lazy H really were the family that had lived in the same block with Dinny and her parents until four years ago.

Dinny did not remember Mike, Janet's brother, too well as he was a year older than she, but Janet! Why, she and Jan had been good friends. How wonderful to have her back!

"I feel the way a kettle must when it is about to boil," Dinny told herself. She tried hard to keep from hurrying, but by the time she reached the top of the hill she was almost running. She stopped to catch her breath.

The ranch was the same as it had always been—house, barn, stall house and tack room, with the rail fence closing the square—but, as Dinny stood there, she saw there was trouble near the stable.

Two horses were tied to the fence. Another had pulled loose and was wandering around, neighing crossly at his trailing lines, which he kept stepping on. In the yard, five people stood waiting for their horses to be saddled.

At the far end of the rail a girl was trying to saddle Winky, a pony.

"That must be Janet," Dinny thought.

Each time the girl tried to put the little saddle on the pony, Winky stepped out of the way.

"Crowd him to the rail," Dinny said, forgetting that Janet could not hear her. "Let him know who is boss!"

As Janet picked up the saddle for the fourth time, Dinny heard a frightening sound—the hollow drumming of hoofs against the walls of a box stall. Then came a voice, half commanding and half begging, "Whoa, now . . . easy, boy . . . hold it, now . . . easy!" Through the stall house door burst a tall boy pulling a plunging horse.

"That must be Mike," Dinny thought, before she realized what was going on. Then she stopped thinking and stared in horror.

Everything happened at once. The horse pulled back, rearing up on his hind legs. Mike held on to the lines. With an angry neigh the horse reared again, narrowly missing Mike with his front hoofs. A woman ran out of the house, screaming, "Mike! Mike!" A man flung himself out the tack room door. The horses at the rail strained at their lines. One of the waiting women, trying to get out of the way, tripped and fell.

Dinny began to run as fast as she could down the hill to the stable. And as she ran she called, "Let go! Let go of that horse!"

It seemed to Dinny that one second she was at the top of the hill, the next second down in the stable yard. "Let go!" she cried again. Mike let the lines drop. The horse turned, shaking his head, then calmly trotted back to the stall house.

For a moment everyone stood stock still. Mike broke the spell. "Thanks." He breathed a long sigh of relief. "Thanks a lot. A whole lot!"

The man who had come out of the tack room rushed to help the upset woman to her feet. The woman who had run out of the house sank down on the porch steps and mopped her forehead. Dinny followed Prince, the horse with which Mike had been arguing, into the stall house.

By the time she came back out, Mike had succeeded in getting Winky's saddle on. Janet was talking to a customer. Going over to Mike, Dinny explained, "You gave Prince the wrong bit. That one is too small. It hurts."

Blushing a color that almost matched his red hair, Mike said, "Well—thanks again. Say, how did you happen to turn up at the right moment? Who are you, anyway?"

Janet was free now and ran over in time to answer Mike's question. "She's Diane Stoner, Mike. Don't you remember? She's Dinny! Oh, Dinny, I am so glad to see you!"

Dinny felt herself smiling from ear to ear as she said happily, "Me too, Jan."

Mike's face broke into a grin that seemed to make his eyes an even brighter blue. "Dinny? Honest? Little Skinny-Dinny—isn't that what I used to call you?"

Janet tugged at Dinny's arm. "Come on and say hello to Mom." She drew Dinny over to the porch. "Mom, you remember Dinny."

Janet's mother smiled. "Of course I do. It is very good to see you again, Dinny dear."

Dinny had that sudden, empty feeling that came so often since her mother died. She remembered that her mother and Mrs. Macklin had been close friends. They used to sit chatting in the back yard at home while she and Janet played with dolls under the oak tree. How long ago that seemed!

"I am just getting over my fright," Mrs. Macklin went on. "That horse Mike was trying to control looked so big and wild! Thanks to you it turned out all right, but I would not want to live through many such moments!"

"Prince is really very gentle," Dinny said, "but . . ."

Before she could finish, she heard her name called and she turned to see Mr. Macklin come striding across the stable yard.

"Dinny? This *is* Dinny, isn't it?"

"Yes, this is Dinny, Dad," Jan said, "and she got here just in time."

"Say, do you know anything about this place?" Mr. Macklin suddenly asked. "Where things are kept, which are the safest horses?" He was hot and worried.

Dinny nodded eagerly. "Oh, yes I do! I have been riding here for ages. I know the place backwards."

"Then would you come and show me? If I don't get these people on the trail soon, I won't *have* any business. You come too, Jan." Looking relieved, he rushed off again with Dinny and Janet right behind him.

For the next quarter of an hour the stable hummed with activity. Mike and Mr. Mac—Dinny had fallen back into calling him that, just as she had years before—managed pretty well, once in a while asking Dinny a question.

Janet, though, followed close on Dinny's heels. "The horses scare me," she confessed. "They are so big and—and bossy!"

Dinny laughed. "They certainly are. And that's just what you can't let them be. There can be only one boss, and you are it. Have you ever baby-sat, Jan?"

Janet nodded.

"Well, you don't have to be cross with little children, but you do have to be firm. Or else they walk all over you to see how much you will let them get away with. It is exactly the same with horses."

A few moments later Mr. Mac asked, "Dinny, how about this horse for a man who says he is a pretty fair rider?"

Dinny moved closer to take a better look at the brown and white spotted horse. "No, that is Comanche. He does not like men. Better take the other paint pony, Apache. Men or women—it's all the same to him."

Seeing the surprised look on Janet's face, she explained, "Horses have their likes and dislikes, just as people do. For instance, Dreamdust is crazy about one particular saddle blanket. She sulks if you put a different one on her."

"Which is Dreamdust?" Janet wanted to know.

Dinny led her down the runway between the stalls. "Here she is. Hi, Dreamy!" When the little mare heard Dinny's voice she began to neigh softly. "Listen! She is talking to me. Dreamdust and I have been riding together for ages. We are friends."

Entering the stall, Dinny reached into her pocket for a lump of sugar. "Here, Dreamdust. Oh, I am so glad to be back!" Then, to Janet, "Come on in. She won't hurt you. Don't be afraid."

Janet edged a little closer, stopping short of the stall. "I—I don't think I ought to. She doesn't know me yet. My, she is such a pretty color!"

"That is strawberry roan," Dinny explained. "Listen, Jan!" Dinny said, and then poured out the story of her Dreamdust Fund and the agreement she had had with Mr. Baron about buying the mare. "Of course, *now* . . ."

"Oh, I know Dad would make a fair agreement," Jan assured her. "He is so crazy for horses, he will understand what you've been trying to do."

"Do you really think . . . ?"

Just then Mike called, "Dinny, come here!" Edging out past Dreamdust, she went down the runway. Mike was standing by Prince's stall. "Mind telling me which bit this horse prefers?"

Dinny's eyes twinkled. "Oh, he's not particular. Just one big enough so it doesn't hurt his mouth."

A few minutes later the riding party, following Mr. Mac's lead on Prince, started down the trail. When Mike had closed the gate behind them, Mrs. Mac called, "Come on up—there's lemonade and cookies."

Dinny and Jan sat on the steps. Mike pulled up a chair for his mother, then perched on the railing.

"It's wonderful, your being here!" Dinny said. "When I got the notice saying you were the new owners of the

29

Lazy H—well, I can't remember being so happy in ages!"
She had been so caught up in her own delight it took
a minute for Dinny to realize it was not entirely shared by
the others. She looked from Jan to Mike to Mrs. Mac in
surprise. "Aren't *you* happy?"

"Well . . ." Mike began.

"It scares me," Janet whispered.

Mrs. Mac looked at Dinny. "You see," she explained,
"when we first heard we had been left this place, it seemed
like the answer to our prayers. Mr. Mac had been sick,
we had no income and the doctor's bills had eaten up
every cent we had saved."

She stopped to smile proudly at her children. "Jan and
Mike were wonderful. Mike worked in a supermarket Sat-
urdays and two evenings a week. It is a wonder that he
kept up with his school work, but his grades did not go
down one bit. As for Jan, she not only baby-sat, but she
did a lot of the work around the house so I would be free
to nurse Mr. Mac. Both Mike and Janet learned that
when something goes wrong, when there's a real crisis,
one can manage to do just about anything needed to meet
the situation.

"Well, anyway, Dinny, when Mr. Mac was getting
better, the doctor said he would have to find a job out
of doors."

"That is when the letter arrived telling us the Lazy H
had been left to Dad," Janet put in.

30

"Golly, I bet you could hardly believe it," Dinny said.

"At first, we couldn't," Mrs. Mac answered.

"Then what is wrong?" Dinny asked.

Mrs. Mac shook her head. "The place is in such bad shape. It needs so many things done to it, things that cost money we don't have. Then, none of us knows the first thing about running a riding stable. For that matter, neither Jan nor I have ever ridden. Look what happened this morning. Everything went wrong. And even if one of us does not have a serious accident—well, suppose we fail?"

"Why," Dinny thought, "she is really frightened!"

"Look, you just can't even think of failing," she heard herself say, to her own surprise. "Think about succeeding, and you will. I know an awful lot about the Lazy H after all this time. I will help all I can."

Dinny found Mike looking at her. His eyes were warm with something she had never seen in a boy's eyes before. "Mike is going to be my friend," she thought. A warmth grew in her and spilled over into a quick smile when Mike said, "Sure—listen, Mom, with Dinny to show us the ropes, we will make out fine."

At that moment a car pulled into the yard. "More customers!" Mike crowed. He slid off the porch rail, calling back to Dinny, "Come on, if you meant what you said about helping. Up and at them—the Lazy H is a going business!"

For the rest of that day, it looked as if Mike might be

right. It was nearly dinner time before the last riders drove away.

As Dinny, Mike and Mr. Mac left the stable after feeding the horses, Mr. Mac reached out to ruffle Dinny's hair. "Don't know what we would have done without you today. She was great—wasn't she, Mike?"

Mike pretended to think it over. "Well, not great. Just good. We don't want to give the girl a swelled head." But his grin told Dinny what he really thought.

"I had better be going," Dinny said with regret. "Daddy worries when I am out after dark. I will come back Monday, though—if you want me."

"You are welcome Monday and every other day," Mr. Mac said as he walked toward the road with Dinny. "We tease a lot, we Macklins," he went on, "but believe me, Dinny, we are grateful to you. Only one thing troubles me. If this keeps up, we will be taking advantage of you, and I don't like that. If I could afford to, I would put you on salary, but I just do not have the money, and that is a fact. I hope you'll explain this to your father." He paused, and then went on eagerly, "The only thing I *can* offer is this—if you really want to give us a hand, you can ride Dreamdust as often and as long as you want, free of charge, as a kind of salary."

"Now," Dinny thought, "I can tell Mr. Mac about my Dreamdust Fund." But suddenly she was ashamed. "Oh, no—this would be the worst possible time to talk about that! It would be taking advantage of Mr. Mac's gratitude. He would feel he would have to say yes because I am helping him." So instead she said, "I would love to. Working at the Lazy H is not really work for me. And—oh, I missed you all such a lot!

"Of course, I will have to ask Daddy," she added, in a low voice. She looked down at her clothes. "He says that when I am in this outfit he cannot tell whether he has a daughter or a son. I—I think I am sort of a disappointment to Daddy," she said, somehow knowing Mr. Mac would understand. "I mean, Mom was so beautiful and all. Dad wants me to be like her."

Mr. Mac's arm dropped around her shoulders. "Honey, your mother *was* beautiful. You, Dinny, are very much like her. Beauty is not a matter of clothes or how you wear your hair or things like that. Those things are just ornaments, like balls on the Christmas tree. Beauty grows from the inside out."

He gave Dinny a quick squeeze. "Now you run along. By the way, tell your Dad I will call him as soon as I get squared away out here."

At the top of the hill, Dinny paused for one last look. Thoughts crowded her head. "The Lazy H has stopped being just a riding stable. It is a—a *home*. A real home, with a whole family happy at being together, not just a house but a place to live."

Turning away, she told herself, "Daddy can't help the

33

way our house is now, so dark and quiet and—and empty, even when both of us are there. The awful thing is, I can't help it either. It's just that it takes a *whole* family to *be* a family."

She quickened her steps. Her father would be waiting for her. He cooked the meals on Saturday. That was her day off. Tomorrow was Sunday, the day she and her father always spent together. And after that, Monday—and the Lazy H again. Something—doesn't everyone *need* something?—to look forward to! Something warm and good.

"If only Daddy will agree to Mr. Mac's plan! He has to, he just has to!"

CHAPTER 3

"Spoiled Brat!"

It was Sunday evening. Dinny and her father sat at a table on their porch, with a deck of cards and two nearly empty glasses of lemonade between them.

Mr. Stoner pushed back his chair, smiling with affection. "The winner—and still champion! Suppose the office hears that you beat me like this? They will be saying, *If Stoner cannot beat his own daughter at playing cards, is he worth his salary?*"

Dinny returned his smile warmly. Sometimes—not often enough, but sometimes—it was like this between them. The way it used to be, all the time, before Mom died. But so often, since then, Dad would be wrapped in his own thoughts, more like a stranger than a father.

Dinny laughed. "At least, Daddy," she said, "they will

35

know you are honest, that you wouldn't cheat to win a card game. More lemonade?"

Mr. Stoner shook his head. "No, thanks. Anything special planned for tomorrow, Dinny?"

Now was her chance. "I have been offered a job," Dinny began. "No, wait. I know you will say that you won't have me working and keeping house, both. But this is not a regular job." Seeing her father's quick frown, she rushed on. "Remember, I told you some people named Macklin had been left the Lazy H?"

"Yes, I remember." Then his face lighted up. "You mean it *is* Hub and Gloria Macklin—the ones who used to live down the block? Well, what do you know!"

Quickly, Dinny filled him in on the Macklin family history to date. "So that's why they simply have to make a go of it," she finished. "And I can help, Dad."

Her father was silent for a moment. At last he said slowly, "Sure, I am all for your lending the Macklins a hand. But your being so crazy over horses worries me. The only clothes I ever see you in, except on Sundays, are those boots and jeans and shirts." His face broke into a grin. "Darn it, girls ought to smell like roses, not stables!"

"*You ought to smell the way your mother used to, and look the way she used to*—that's what he is thinking," Dinny told herself. "But I can't. I am not Mom. I am me, and I have to *be* me. I *cannot* be anyone else."

She wished, for a moment, that she could say it out

loud to her father. Maybe it would clear the air between them, help them understand each other. But she could not bring herself to put it into words. Instead, she said, "Dad, would you agree to my working at the Lazy H for a short while, until you see what it is like and make up your mind? It is not just the horses. It's the Macklins. And it is not only that they need me, but I like being with them. Please, Daddy, don't be hurt, but it's—it's *quiet* here when you are not home."

"Sure. Sure, honey. You go ahead. Do as you like." He got to his feet. "I brought some papers home to look over. Goodnight."

Watching him go, Dinny thought, "We are right back where we started. Nothing has changed." But one thing, at least, was changed. Tomorrow there was the Lazy H to go to, Dreamdust to ride . . .

Next morning, Dinny was out at the ranch by eight. Everyone was busy—Mrs. Mac was making a batch of doughnuts, Janet was tidying up the kitchen, Mike was leading a party of early riders, and Mr. Mac was cleaning the stall house. Dinny pitched in to help him.

As they worked their way the length of the building, Mr. Mac paused by Dreamdust's stall. "Pretty little thing, isn't she? No wonder she is your favorite, Dinny."

"She is more than my favorite," Dinny said.

And with that beginning it was not hard to tell the rest—the plan she had to buy Dreamdust, how hard she had worked to save the money, how worried she had been when she heard the stable might be passing into new hands. Dinny hoped Mr. Mac would understand.

"You would still like to buy her, right? Well, from this moment on Dreamdust has a big *Reserved for Dinny* sign around her neck!"

Dinny tried to thank him, but she could not find the right words. All she could say was "Thank you, Mr. Mac," before she turned and continued sweeping the stall house.

Few customers showed up that day, so there was plenty of time in the afternoon for Mrs. Mac and Jan to take their first riding lessons.

Although Mrs. Mac was not "horse crazy," as she teased Dinny and Mike about being, she liked them well enough. More important, she was not one bit afraid.

"No beast is going to get the better of me," she gasped, bouncing around in the saddle, "so this one had better not try!" Sure enough, she quickly learned to let her body move in time with the movements of the horse.

"That's half the battle, riding Western style," Mr. Mac said, encouragingly.

Janet, though, was terrified. Dinny and Mike had to do a lot of talking to persuade her to get up on the horse at all. Once in the saddle she closed her eyes tight and moaned, "What if she bucks?"

Dinny could not help laughing. "Little Sister? She is the slowest, laziest horse in the United States. She hasn't bucked since she was a colt—which was probably about the time of the Civil War! Go ahead, now. Kick her in the ribs, the way I told you, to get her started."

Janet's eyes flew open. "*Kick* her? She will hate me. She will *never* let me ride her then."

Mike took a turn. "Not with all your might, for Pete's sake. Just a good, firm poke. She has been trained to expect it. Go ahead, now. Give her a little kick with both heels and tell her . . ." He turned to Dinny. "What do you say to make Little Sister move?"

Dinny laughed. "She will move for *Hup!* if you sound as if you mean business."

Finally, Jan was persuaded to try. She kicked—lightly. She said *Hup!*—softly. Little Sister remained where she was. "That sounded like a nothing," Mike said. "Try again—as if you mean it!"

Janet tried again. Dinny added a louder, firmer "Hup, Little Sister—hup!" Mike gave her a slap on the side. Little Sister thought it over, sighed, took a dozen slow steps and stopped. To everyone's surprise Janet burst into tears.

Dinny's patience gave way. "Oh honestly! Janet, you great big *baby!* You ought to be ashamed!"

Little Sister had had enough nonsense for one day. She started for the stall house at a slow walk, Janet sliding limply around on her back.

Dinny's anger changed to anxiety. "Duck!" she cried

to Janet. "Keep your head down!" She began to run.

Hearing rushing steps behind her, Little Sister rushed, too. She was not going fast, really. Just fast enough not to be caught. Just fast enough so that if Jan did not duck, her head was sure to hit the low door frame!

But then, at the last possible second, Little Sister stopped. *Well*, she seemed to say, *don't just sit there. Get off! You don't want to be there, so get off!*

Mr. Mac had come hurrying up. "Little Sister has more

sense than all three of you together!" When his daughter was safely on the ground he told her, "Nobody should be forced to learn to ride," he said to Jan. "We will wait till you *want* to learn. You will want to, honey, because you will miss too much if you don't—trail picnics, moonlight rides, all sorts of fun. When you are ready, tell me and we will start over. All right?"

He turned to Dinny and Mike. "Things are slow this afternoon. Why don't you explore some of the trails?"

Delighted by the idea, Mike disappeared into the stall house. Dinny followed more slowly. "That was my fault," she thought. "Me and my darned temper! Why can't I hang on to it? I want Jan to learn to ride, to enjoy it as much as I do, and now I have fixed it so she probably will never get on a horse again as long as she lives! That's the way it always happens—I want something, and right away I spoil it."

Mike had Dreamdust saddled for her by the time she reached the far end of the stall house. "I think I will try Comanche this trip," he said. "Might as well get familiar with as many of the horses as I can."

"Why not take Apache? He is the other paint pony."

A certain look came into Mike's blue eyes. "Why not Comanche? I'm a pretty good rider, you know."

"I know you are, Mike," Dinny said softly. "Actually, Apache is the harder horse to handle. It is just that Comanche doesn't like men. He always plays tricks."

But Mike would not change his mind. He would ride Comanche, if only to prove he could handle any horse. Besides, what made Dinny think she knew everything?

"I will show Comanche that I am the boss," Mike told her firmly.

As the two riders started down the trail, it seemed as if Mike were right. Comanche gave no trouble. Mike was very pleased with himself.

"Just you wait and see," Dinny said—but not out loud. Mike would have to learn the hard way.

When they were out of sight of the ranch, Mike slowed Comanche to a walk. He no longer thought about the horse's temper. "Dinny, listen—what do you think? Can we make a go of the Lazy H?" He was deadly serious.

"I really don't know," Dinny answered slowly. "The only other stable between here and the city is Cottonwood Hills, and that is much too fancy and expensive for the people who ride at the Lazy H. So actually there's no competition." She hesitated, then plunged ahead. "But nobody has bothered about the Lazy H for so long! Mr. Baron let the whole place fall to pieces—you can see that for yourself. And he was so rude that he drove most of the customers away."

"Doesn't sound promising, does it?" Mike answered. "If only we had the money to tell people there is a new deal here, that would help." He sighed. "Well, we can only try. And believe me, it will be a big try."

Mike was silent for a moment. "One thing bothers me. Mom and Dad want me to go back to Locust Valley in the fall for my senior year of high. To be perfectly honest, I want to go, too. I have a good chance to be right end on the football team, and I play pretty fair basketball, and—well, you know how it is. You want to finish high school where you started, where you know everybody."

"I am sure he has a steady girl there," Dinny thought, as Mike stared straight ahead, lost in himself. Dinny wondered why she felt so sad and lonely.

Suddenly, Mike spoke up. "Tell me more about this fancy Cottonwood Hills place."

"A Colonel Gill owns it. He is an old army man, so everything is done in a very set way. I don't like it at all. Riding is for fun, or why ride? Of course, you do learn a lot," Dinny went on, trying to be fair. "Hunting and jumping—almost anything you want to learn."

"How do you know so much about it?" Mike asked.

"Oh, I have a friend, Lissa Lambert, who rides there. I have gone with her a few times—as her guest. Her folks have money. Lissa is very nice, though. And is she pretty! Wait till you see her!"

Mike made no comment on that. For a while they rode in silence, until they came to a stream. "Watch yourself crossing here," Dinny warned. "This is one of the places where Comanche shows how he feels about men riders."

"Don't worry," Mike told her in a superior way. "Comanche and I are getting along fine. See what I mean?"

Dinny urged Dreamdust across the stream. When the mare had picked her way to the other side, Dinny turned so that she could watch Mike. Following Dreamdust, Comanche started to cross the stream. "If I were you, Mike," Dinny suggested quietly, "I would get my feet loose and be ready to jump."

Mike gave her a startled look and then took her advice —almost too late. With that peculiar sound from which the term "horse laugh" comes, Comanche slid into the water, for all the world like a person letting himself down into a bathtub. Mike did jump away, but not quickly enough to land on shore. He found himself sitting up to his waist in water, with two horses and a girl laughing at him. He did not even try to get up.

For a moment, Mike glared at Dinny. Then he, too, began to laugh. "All right, say it! You told me so!"

They returned to the ranch, where Mike changed his clothes. Dinny led Comanche back to his stall, entertaining Mr. Mac with the story of how Mike lost his argument with the horse.

"Where is Apache?" she asked, seeing the next stall empty.

"A young man has him out. A Bud Winslow."

Dinny bent down to loosen the buckle on the strap that held Comanche's saddle in place, but, suddenly, she stood up straight and looked at Mr. Mac.

"Bud Winslow? Did you say Bud Winslow? Did he go out alone?"

Mr. Mac was leaning against the corner post, mopping his forehead.

"He said he was a good rider, and, well, I just didn't feel up to going along. Do you know him, Dinny?"

Dinny nodded. "Yes, I know him, and he is a good rider. But he is not—oh, not such a good person. His father is something important in politics in Carney's Landing—you know, the little town over toward the river? Bud's a show-off. Even Colonel Gill at Cottonwood had trouble with him."

At that point, two customers turned up. Mike, in dry clothes, took them out.

"If you want to go lie down a while," Dinny suggested to Mr. Mac, "I will take over."

Mr. Mac nodded. "I will do just that." He reached out to ruffle her hair. "Thanks, Dinny."

Dinny went to work in the tack room, trying to bring some order there. About an hour later, the sound of pounding hoofs and a roaring, "Whoa! Pull up!" sent her flying out to the stable yard. There was Bud Winslow, getting off a horse.

And there was Apache, a sorry mess. The horse was breathing fast and he was covered with lather—the white sweat-like foam which is a sure sign that a horse has been ridden too far, too fast, too hard.

45

There was a second when Dinny felt too small to hold the big, hot anger inside her. Then words came, spilling out in double time.

"Look at that horse! Just *look!* You have ridden Apache right into the ground!"

"So what? I pay to ride, don't I? So I can ride any way I want to!" Bud said.

"You can't ride any way you want to, not at Cottonwood and not here either!"

"What difference does it make to you?" Bud asked. "You don't own this ranch. Besides, it's only a horse."

"*Only* a horse?" Dinny's voice rose high.

Suddenly, Bud laughed. "You are cute when you're mad, Dinny."

That did it. Dinny's temper exploded. "Get out! Get out! And don't you ever dare come back!"

Bud's face, flaming red, took on an ugly look. "All right, all right! But you listen to me, Dinny Stoner. I won't be back—and neither will any of my friends. I will spread the word all over Carney's Landing!"

Watching Bud tear out of the yard in his little sports car, Dinny had a sick feeling in place of her anger.

"My temper—always my temper!" she thought. "Won't I ever learn? Customers are what the Lazy H needs most. Mr. Mac tries to think up ways to get new ones—and I drive the old ones away! I want to help, but everything turns out just the opposite!"

46

CHAPTER 4

Double Trouble

Late that afternoon, when Bud's father telephoned to complain about how his son had been treated, Mr. Mac backed Dinny up. He told Mr. Winslow a few things that should have made Bud's ears burn. But that was small comfort to Dinny.

"If Bud does keep his friends away," she thought, "that will be—well, just too bad! Business has to pick up soon. It has to get better and better every day, or there won't be a Lazy H much longer."

But business did not pick up. The rest of that week was no better than Monday, and the following week was even worse. Most of the regulars from Carney's Landing had stopped coming, just as Bud had said they would. Then a family of five faithful riders moved away from Springfield.

And finally two sisters, who had ridden at the Lazy H twice each week, went out of town for the summer.

"If business were normal those few would not matter," Mr. Mac told Dinny and his family one morning when they had stopped for a coffee break. "But as things are, each lost rider is a disaster."

Mike, who was looking out the window, gave a long, low whistle. "Maybe our luck has changed. Look!" Four heads turned. A long low car had parked in the yard. A tall older man and a slim blonde girl got out of the car. She hated to, but Dinny had to throw cold water on the excitement.

"Those are not customers. The man is Colonel Gill—you know, the owner of Cottonwood Hills. The girl is my friend, Lissa Lambert."

Followed by the three young people, Mr. Mac went out to greet the visitors. As they crossed the yard Dinny heard Jan whisper to her brother, with a little laugh, "That's a girl, Mike. My goodness, didn't you ever see a girl before?"

Stealing a quick glance, Dinny saw that Mike's mouth had fallen open. She almost laughed—but the laughter stuck in her throat.

She had seen that expression on boys' faces before when they looked at Lissa, and she had always thought it was funny. Now, Dinny told herself, it was about the least funny thing she could think of.

48

"No boy has ever looked at me that way," she thought, "and most likely no boy ever will. I didn't care before, but now I do . . ."

While Mike was looking at Lissa and Dinny was looking at both of them, Mr. Mac and the colonel met and walked toward the stall house. Lissa, wearing her best smile, joined the others. After Dinny had introduced Mike and Jan, Lissa explained the visit.

"Colonel Gill wants to buy some horses. I persuaded him to come here," she said, talking to Mike.

"Jan and I might as well be invisible," Dinny thought.

Still paying no attention to the girls, Lissa chatted in her pretty, bird-song voice. "I want to see everything! Please show me around, Mike?"

"Sure," Mike gulped, grinned, fished around in his mind for something else to say. "Sure. Sure, I will."

Dinny decided it was time someone else took a hand. "You have seen it all, Lissa. Nothing is changed."

For a moment Lissa looked so disappointed that Jan and Dinny had all they could do to keep from laughing. But it didn't take her long to compose herself.

"Mike, isn't Dinny just *wonderful?* I mean, pitching right in, grooming horses and cleaning stalls and all? I always say, there is nobody like Dinny! Why, she is as good as a boy when it comes to hard work. If I did half what she does, I would drop dead!"

Dinny's face flamed. "I—I have w-work to do," she

managed to say, and rushed off before anyone saw the tears that stung her eyes.

When she was safely inside the barn, she found Janet right behind her. "That—that *female!*" Jan cried. "She can go and drop dead any time she wants to. And that brother of mine! Did you see the soupy look on his face?"

Dinny laughed, then quickly grew serious. "The thing is, Jan, Lissa's right. I *can* work hard. I *am* as handy to have around as any boy. But I will never get a boy to look at me the way Mike is looking at Lissa right now!" She gave a grim laugh. "Oh, well. I guess I'll go clean out the box stalls. Each to his own trade, I always say!"

Dinny plunged into her work. Mr. Mac and Colonel Gill walked through the stall house twice, pausing to look at each horse. Dinny paid them no attention. Even when Mike and Lissa came down the runway she determined not to listen. But neither the bright sound of Lissa's voice nor Mike's deep laughter escaped her.

When she reached the end stall, Dinny heard the men talking outside the door. She did not intend to, but she could not help hearing a few words—and then, fear making her heart beat double time, she stopped and really listened.

"That's how it is," Colonel Gill was saying. "Most of your stock is no use to me. They are quarter horses, Western trained. But the big bay, Prince, and the little mare, Dreamdust, suit me perfectly. I have made you a fair offer, Mr. Macklin. What do you say?"

Dinny caught her breath. "He won't sell Prince," she thought. "Prince is his own favorite. And Dreamdust—oh, he *couldn't* sell Dreamdust!"

"I have told you how things are here at the Lazy H," she heard Mr. Mac reply. "We are operating on a shoestring. The money those two horses would bring could give us a little something to build up business. From that point of view, it does not seem as if I could afford not to sell you Prince and Dreamdust."

Dinny felt as if the world had come to an end. She whirled and ran down the runway. Quickly throwing Dreamdust's blanket and saddle on, she mounted the mare and, lying low on her neck, rode her out of the stall house. She urged her into a trot, then into a gallop.

"I won't let anyone have you!" she told Dreamdust, as she turned her into the woods. "You are mine!"

Dinny kept up the pace until they were far down the trail. Then, suddenly, she pulled the mare to a halt as they reached a small, open area. Leaning forward to stroke Dreamdust's neck, she told her, "I'm sorry, Dreamy. I was riding you too hard, wasn't I?" She slid down from the saddle and let the horse crop the tender grass at the edge of a little stream.

After a moment she went on, speaking half to Dreamdust and half to herself. "Wasn't that a silly thing to do, riding off like that? Where did I think it would get me?

Even if you are such a small horse, I can't very well hide you in the guest room at home!"

Dinny tried to laugh at her own joke, but there was no room for laughter in her then. She felt sick. What would the Lazy H be without Dreamdust? What would her life be without the little horse who was her constant friend?

Sunk in her gloomy thoughts, Dinny did not hear the quiet thud of another horse's hoofs on the soft grass. She did not realize she was no longer alone until a voice called her name softly. Startled, she turned to see Mr. Mac getting down from Prince.

He came across the grass to her, smiling. "Remember the old joke about the farmer who lost a cow? He asked himself, *Where would I go if I were a cow?* and he went there—and there was his cow. I asked myself, *Where would I go if I were frightened and unhappy, as Dinny is now?* I thought of this little spot, with the stream running through it—and here you are. Dinny?"

"Yes, Mr. Mac?" Raising her eyes to his face, she saw how worried Mr. Mac looked. Dinny suddenly felt very much ashamed. "Oh, Mr. Mac, I'm sorry! I wasn't thinking about anyone but myself. I know you wouldn't sell Dreamdust unless you absolutely *had* to!"

"Who said anything about selling Dreamdust?"

Dinny stared at him in surprise. "W-why, you did," she burst out. "I mean, I heard you tell Colonel . . ."

"You know what happens to people who listen in on

someone else's conversation?" Mr. Mac's voice was severe, but there was a twinkle in his eyes that Dinny could not understand. "They hear no good, remember? Now, what was it you heard, young lady?"

Completely puzzled, Dinny fumbled in her mind for the exact words. "You—yes, you said, 'It does not seem as if I could afford not . . . not to sell Prince and Dreamdust.'"

Mr. Mac nodded. "That's what I said. The trouble is, you didn't stay long enough to hear what I said next. I told the colonel that, afford it or not, I wouldn't sell those horses. Prince is my best horse, and he is also my favorite. As for Dreamdust, I have given you my word that you can buy her. I can't go back on my word."

Tears of joy filled Dinny's eyes. She was too overcome to say a word. Mr. Mac himself was moved. Smiling, he commanded, "Now stop that! Dry your eyes, Dinny. Why women cry when they are happy is beyond me."

Dinny gave Mr. Mac a quick hug. "Thank you—oh, thank you so much! Golly, I want to be a help to you, and instead I cause you a lot of trouble."

Mr. Mac reached out to ruffle her hair in his familiar gesture of affection. "Don't worry, Dinny. You are a joy to have around, and I really mean that. Now let's get on our horses and get back home, shall we?"

They rode back to the ranch in silence. At the gate, Mr. Mac slowed his horse. "You know what, Dinny? I

53

have a feeling in my bones. I think things are going to start looking up from now on. I don't know why, but—well, I just feel it. So hold your breath. I honestly think the Lazy H is on its way!"

As day followed day and added up to a week, then two weeks, it seemed as if Mr. Mac were right. It was perfect riding weather, sunny during the day with a shower nearly every night to keep the dust settled. New customers began to come. Not as many as there should have been, "But enough," as Mr. Mac put it, "to keep our heads above water. That's all I ask, right now."

Those were happy days for Dinny. The work of getting the stable into running order was done, and that left a little time for fun. Several afternoons Jan and Mike and Dinny found time to go swimming at a small lake near the ranch. One Saturday, Dinny's father kept his promise to come and inspect the Lazy H, and to renew his friendship with the Macklins.

On the way home Mr. Stoner told Dinny, "I don't remember when I have enjoyed myself so much. You are right, honey—the Lazy H is a great place for you to spend your days this summer. Forget I ever had any objections, and just go ahead and have fun."

So that was one problem solved, Dinny thought.

Another one was taken care of a few days later. The night before, Mr. Mac and Mike and Dinny had taken a group of riders on a moonlight ride along the dark, pine trails. The next morning they talked about it so much that Jan told her father, "I guess you were right, Dad. I am going to miss a lot, not being able to ride. I would like to try again."

This time, Mr. Mac did the teaching himself. Janet was still nervous about the horses, still could not bring herself to trust them. But she made some progress. She rode slow and gentle Little Sister, and if the two did not really understand each other, at least girl and horse learned to get along with each other.

For Dinny, the only cloud in the sky of those pleasant weeks was Lissa Lambert. After all her talk about English being the only way to ride, Lissa developed a burning interest in Western.

"No, face it," Dinny told herself, "Lissa's burning interest is really in Mike. And believe me, he returns it." To Dinny, Lissa looked slightly silly in her handsome riding habit, mounted on a quarter horse and trying to post in a Western saddle. But Mike did not notice. "In fact," Dinny thought, "about all Mike does notice these days is Lissa herself. . . ."

One morning, while she and Mike were doing their stable cleaning, Dinny said, "I think something nice is going to happen, Mike. Like new customers, maybe. Not just one or two, but a whole lot."

Mike grinned at her. "Getting feelings in your bones, like Dad?" Suddenly, Janet burst in, eyes wide open.

"Girls!" Jan gasped. "Some girls who want to start a riding club. They want to start it *here!*"

Mike's eyes met Dinny's. "You ever think of taking up fortune telling?" he asked her. Then, to his sister, "Lead me to them, Jan."

It was ten minutes or so, a very long ten minutes for Dinny, before Mike returned. She could tell from his face that the news was good. "Twelve girls!" he shouted. "Count them—a round dozen! They want to ride once a week, starting this Friday. How do you like that?"

"I like it. I like it fine!"

Mike caught Dinny's hand. "Come on, let's tell the others. This is too good to keep to ourselves another

minute!" Hand in hand they ran across the stable yard and tore into the house by the kitchen door.

Mr. and Mrs. Mac, alerted by Jan, were waiting. "Is it true?" Mrs. Mac asked in an anxious voice. "A riding club? How many are there?"

It was Mike's story, and Dinny let him tell it. When he had finished, Dinny turned dancing eyes to Mr. Mac. "Is it safe for me to let my breath out now?"

He pretended to think it over seriously. "Not yet," he decided. "Ask me again a week from today and I will give you an answer."

The days flew. It was Friday before they knew it. At ten in the morning the riding club turned up. "They are

even on time," Mike whispered to Dinny. "Look at them —twelve live customers! What a beautiful sight!"

"It's only because they are girls," his sister teased. "If it were a boys' riding club you wouldn't be so happy."

"Listen," Mike assured her, "each of those girls could have two heads, and I would still be crazy for her. Come on, let's show our club some snappy Lazy H service!"

With Mr. Mac, on Prince, leading the way and Mike, on Apache, bringing up the rear, the long procession rode out at ten-thirty. Dinny went to the stall house to put more hay in the boxes. As she often did when there was no one else around, she talked to Dreamdust. "I heard one of the girls say the club would probably ride twice a week in the fall. You know, Dreamy, if we could dig up more riding clubs, we could stop worrying."

Dinny had just finished with the hay when she heard Mike calling her. Something must have happened, something bad, to make Mike leave the riding club in charge of one guide, especially this first time! She ran out. Mike was leading Apache slowly across the stable yard.

"What's wrong?" Dinny asked in an anxious voice.

Mike shook his head. "Don't know for sure. Apache's sick. I walked him back."

Together, Dinny and Mike ran their hands over the horse, searching for cuts or sores. Then Dinny noticed that his nose was running. "And it's all red inside, too," she pointed out. "Mike, what do you suppose is wrong?"

58

"I don't know. But we have to find out. Listen, we can't leave Dad alone with that mob of girls to handle. You take Dreamdust and meet the club up on the ridge trail. I'm going to call Dr. Hansen."

Dinny saddled Dreamdust and rode out, meeting Mr. Mac and his charges on the ridge. He raised his eyebrows at Dinny. She shook her head, trying to make her smile say, *I'm sure it's not worth worrying about.* But she could not help worrying, herself.

An hour later—one of the longest hours in Dinny's memory—she and Mr. Mac brought the riding club back to the stable. There were no more customers at the moment. They found Mike beside Apache's stall.

"Did Dr. Hansen come?" Dinny asked.

"Right away. Within a few minutes after I called."

"What is it, son?" Mr. Mac asked, as Mike hesitated.

"He—he says it might be glanders. Dad, do you know what glanders is?"

Mr. Mac nodded slowly. "Glanders is a terribly dangerous sickness. Other horses can catch it. So can humans. You say the doctor is not certain?"

"No." Mike shook his head. "He took some blood samples to be tested. He can't tell for sure until the tests come back. But Dad—Dad, he says that we must close the stables!"

CHAPTER 5

Until Further Notice

Next morning at breakfast, Dinny told her father what had happened at the Lazy H.

"Mike painted a sign," she finished, "CLOSED UNTIL FURTHER NOTICE. We nailed it to the post that holds the mail box, at the head of the dirt road leading to the stable. Dad, you never saw such sad people in your life. It's a shame—just when everything was beginning to run well at last! Poor Mr. Mac tried to be cheerful, telling us it could not be glanders. But he is just sunk, that's all."

Mr. Stoner took a last sip of his coffee and pushed his chair back. "Glanders? That's a new one on me, Dinny. Just what *is* glanders, anyway? Do you know?"

Dinny wished she did not have to tell him. He was

going to be so worried! But there was no sense trying to keep it a secret. He could find out easily enough. So she said, "I read about it last night in that horse book you gave me last Christmas. It's serious, all right. Very catching, the book says. Besides horses, dogs, goats, sheep and even people can catch it. But not cows. Isn't that funny?"

"Not very," said her father, who was beginning to look troubled. "What else did it say?"

"Well, there is a fever and the inside of the nose becomes bright red—it was the way Apache's nose looked yesterday that made Mike decide we had to call the doctor. There is swelling in some glands, too, and lumps that form under the skin." She hesitated. "It—the book says it often ends in death. Dad, what if the horses *die?* What if Dreamdust should—"

Mr. Stoner leaned forward. "Good heavens, girl, who is going to worry about horses? You have all been exposed to it. You, the Macklins, all the recent riders at the stable—every one of you." He got quickly to his feet. "I am going to call Dr. Rudolph. Stay right here, Dinny."

Waiting for her father to return, Dinny told herself, "I won't think about what *might* happen, all the horses getting it, and Dreamdust. No, that's so terrible it—it just doesn't bear thinking about, that's all. If anything ever happened to Dreamdust!" Then she stopped, ashamed. "Daddy's right—I should not be worrying about what might happen to the horses, when for all I know

61

every single one of us may come down with glanders any minute, and maybe die of it. I have to think about it the other way—that what is wrong isn't glanders at all, and that everything will be all right."

In a few moments her father was back. "What the doctor has to say about glanders is bad, honey—about as bad as it can be. But he says there is not much point keeping you away from the stable. You have already been exposed to the sickness. So go ahead if you want to. They can probably stand cheering up."

"Thanks, Dad. I don't know that I'll be much good as far as cheering them up goes, but I can try. There's a roasting chicken in the icebox if you want to stick it in the oven later. And I made an angel cake last night. Well, I'll be going now."

"Hon, do we have two of those chickens?" her father asked.

"Three. Why, Dad?"

"Well, it suddenly occurred to me that I might go along with you. I don't like to drop in on the Macklins without letting them know, but if we took the chickens and your cake, you and Jan could whip dinner together. Maybe I could help cheer up Hub and Gloria. At least I can be useful. There is still an awful lot to be done to those stables. I don't know much about horses, but I can swing a paint brush with the best of them."

Dinny turned to him, her face glowing. "It's a wonderful idea. You get the chickens and I'll pack up the cake."

On the drive out to the Lazy H, Dinny and her father talked seriously about the Macklins and their problems. "If Hub were well," Mr. Stoner said, "I wouldn't worry. Even if the Lazy H should go out of business, he's a young enough man to start over. But the fact is, he has never completely recovered from that long illness of his. And—well, if the Lazy H should fail, I have an idea he never *would* recover."

"Even if this glanders scare turns out not to be serious at all, just missing the big end-of-the-week business will wipe out all the gains the Lazy H has made these past weeks," Dinny said. "It isn't fair! Trouble ought to be spread around so everybody gets a share!"

Mr. Stoner reached out to pat her hand. "Try telling that to people who are running in *good* luck, Dinny, and you will be about as popular as the measles."

As Mr. Stoner had guessed, not much was going on at the Lazy H. When she learned they had company, Mrs. Mac began to prepare a large pitcher of lemonade, and Dinny's father and Mr. Mac walked around the place to see what needed doing and how much they could get done.

Dinny, checking on the horses, found Mike and Janet in the stall house. Dr. Hansen had already been there, Mike told Dinny. "Whatever it is, Apache and Comet and Mousie and Winky have it. And—"

"No, not Dreamdust," Janet put in, seeing Dinny's anxious eyes travel down to Dreamy's stall. "She is her same old bright self."

"What puzzles Dr. Hansen," Mike continued, "is that the horses don't seem to be sick *enough*. In fact, Apache seems just about well again. The doctor points out that horses seldom recover from glanders, at least not nearly that fast. Besides that—"

"What it boils down to," Janet interrupted, "is he doesn't know, so of course he won't commit himself. We'll just have to wait for the reports from the state health center."

"When will they be back?" Dinny asked.

"That's another thing the doctor can't say for sure. Tuesday, he guesses, but more likely Wednesday." Mike paused, listening. "Isn't that Mom calling us?"

They all gathered on the side porch, where Mrs. Mac had lemonade and cookies waiting.

Dinny's father and Mr. Mac divided up the work they felt needed to be done. Mike would cut and put up new poles to replace those that were broken in the rail fence. Mr. Stoner, with Jan and Dinny, would take over painting the stall house.

"How about you, Hub?"

"I'll patch the tack and mend the reins that have worn through. I found an old shoemakers' kit in the barn. It

has big curved needles, flax thread, wax, and leather strings
—the works. Just what I need."

"I'll come to the tack room with you," Mrs. Mac said,
"and bring my own needles and thread. I can mend and
bind those old saddle blankets."

They worked very hard all day, pausing only for a bite
at lunch time. In the afternoon, Jan and Dinny took
time out to get the chickens in the oven, cut up potatoes,
go down the road to the truck farmer for fresh beans,
salad greens and tomatoes. Then the two girls, with Mike
to help, gave food and water to the horses. After that they

put the finishing touches on dinner and set the table. Finally they called a loud, farm style "Come and get it!"

Dinner was a cheerful meal. Behind them lay a lot of much-needed, well-done work. Ahead of them—well, like Dinny, they all had determined not to let themselves think about that. Worry would not help. They could only wait and see.

When the dishes were cleared away they all sat on the porch in the dark, enjoying the cool breeze, too tired to make conversation. Finally Mr. Stoner said, "Well, Dinny, we had better be on our way." He sounded as though he didn't want to leave, and Dinny was glad. That meant he had enjoyed himself today.

She started to answer, but Mrs. Mac interrupted. "Ed, why don't you and Dinny stay the night? We would love to have you. Anyway, from the sound of your voice you're likely as not to fall fast asleep driving home."

Mr. Stoner was quiet for a second. "What do you say, Dinny? Shall we stay?"

Dinny had learned, a long time ago, to tell by her father's voice whether he really wanted to do whatever he was proposing. Now his tone was just right.

"Oh, I'd love to!" she said, and that was settled. A few minutes after that, hardly able to say goodnight through their yawns, they all went to bed.

Sunday was even more pleasant than Saturday, in spite of the cloud which hung over the Lazy H. Early in the morning they went riding—all of them, even Janet and Mr. Stoner. In fact, Jan gave up her quiet, sturdy friend, Little Sister, so that Dinny's father could ride her, and chose Comanche for herself.

They all ate a huge breakfast and, as before, they did not talk about the troubles. After breakfast, they went to services at the little white church on Chapel Road. And then, the day was like the day before, full of the hard but rewarding job of getting the Lazy H in the best possible shape for "when we open up again."

Finally it was evening again, and this time Dinny and her father did have to leave.

"It's been great of you, Ed," Mr. Mac told Dinny's father. "We probably wouldn't have done much of anything if you hadn't turned up to help us."

He bent down, smiling into the car where Dinny sat. "Fact is, I don't know what we would have done without Dinny all this time. She's a pretty good pusher, herself." The teasing went out of his voice. "She's a fine girl, Ed, your daughter is. You can be proud of her. Reminds me of her mother."

Dinny caught her breath. No matter how good a mood Daddy was in, just the mention of Mom always made him quiet and distant.

But no! Not this time! To her surprise and joy, Dinny heard her father answer, in a perfectly normal tone, "That's certainly true, Hub. I see it myself more and more every day. And believe me, I couldn't ask for anything better for Dinny than that she turn out to be as fine a woman as her mother." He started the engine. "Well, goodnight, Hub. Thanks for a pleasant time."

"The big thanks are due to you. Goodnight now, and safe home." But Mr. Mac didn't move away. He remained there, looking into the car window, not wanting to let them go. Dinny got the feeling there was something more he wanted to say. Or felt he ought to say.

"Don't worry, Hub," Mr. Stoner said. "I have a feeling everything is going to turn out fine. One thing, none of us is sick. From what Dr. Rudolph said, if that were going to happen it should have happened by now."

Mr. Mac's hand reached out to touch his friend's arm. "Ed, that's what I have been trying to get up the nerve to say. I don't want to frighten Gloria and the kids, but I feel somebody ought to know. I'm sick. So . . . well, I guess I'm the first one. All I can hope is that I am the only one!"

CHAPTER 6

News—But Is It Good?

For a moment there was absolute silence. Then Dinny's father got out of the car and rushed Mr. Mac into the house. Mr. Mac did not protest. He seemed so sick that he was glad to let someone else take charge.

Mr. Stoner and Mrs. Mac got Mr. Mac up the stairs and into bed, and Dr. Rudolph was sent for. "I will phone you the minute there is any definite news," Mrs. Mac promised as Dinny and her father started home.

"You know, honey, some people just seem to be born to trouble," Mr. Stoner said as they drove home. "Remember the story about King Midas, who turned everything he touched to gold? Hub Macklin seems to have that gift in reverse. Everything he touches blows right up in his face! I say I don't believe in luck. What happens to you is the result of your being good or bad, strong or weak, hard-working or lazy. Luck has nothing to do with it. Then I see what happens to a man like Hub, a good guy if there ever was one, and I'm not so sure!"

Those words kept turning over and over in Dinny's mind long after she went to bed. Was it true—was there such a thing as luck? And if there was, was Mr. Mac's always going to be bad?

There was no news from the Lazy H by the time Dinny had breakfast on the table next morning. She and her father had little to say during the meal. "I'm stiff," Mr. Stoner said once. "Muscles I didn't even know I had are aching." But Dinny knew his mind was not really on his sore muscles. He knew hers was not either.

"I can't take any more of this," Mr. Stoner said, pushing his chair back from the table. "I'm going to call and see what's what!" But when he came back from talking to Mrs. Mac he had very little to report. "Gloria says Hub feels about the same. The doctor would not commit himself last night as to what the trouble was. He said he would stop by again this morning. Going to the ranch today?"

"Oh, yes. Of course I am," Dinny answered.

Her father shook his head. "I don't know whether you should or not, honey. It's certainly not very cheerful. And after all, fond as you are of the Macklins, these troubles are theirs, not yours."

"Why, they are, too, my troubles," Dinny told him. "The Macklins have treated me just like one of the family—and it has been wonderful being one of the family. I would be pretty low, wouldn't I, if I accepted all the pleasant things being part of the family means, but ran for cover as soon as trouble turned up?"

Mr. Stoner smiled. "That's true—and seeing how you feel about it, I can't very well forbid you to go out there." He took a step nearer. "You know something, Dinny? I *like* you. You are a pretty nice young girl. There was a time when I thought you were all wrapped up in yourself and didn't give a hoot for anybody else. But I was wrong."

Dinny caught her breath and took her courage in both hands. "No, you were right. I have changed. And Daddy— do *you* know what? There was a time when I thought *you* were all wrapped up in yourself and didn't give a hoot about anybody else. Isn't it funny how two people can live together and be as close as we are, and still not under-stand each other very well?"

He gave her a swift hug. "Besides being nice, you are pretty wise for your years. I guess we have both changed, honey. The only thing, I am sorry it took someone else's troubles to make us see that our own are not very im-portant."

After her father was gone, Dinny did the dishes and cleaned up the living room. She was about to leave the house when the phone rang. "It's probably one of the

71

Macklins," she thought, as she rushed to answer. Bad news? Oh, let it be good news for a change!

Dinny was so certain that the call would be from the Lazy H that for a moment she did not recognize the voice that gasped, "Dinny? Oh, I'm so glad I caught you before you left! Dinny, is it true?"

"Who is this? Is what true?"

"This is Lissa, silly! Is it true about the Lazy H? The milkman told our cleaning woman that some of the horses are sick. He says it's *glanders.* Why, that's a horrible disease! Almost always ends in death!"

"Now wait a minute, Lissa Lambert!" Anger steamed up in Dinny and boiled over. "Just you wait a minute! It isn't glanders at all. It is just a—a little germ, no worse than a cold in the head! You had better not go spreading that story around. You could ruin the Lazy H that way, you know that? Don't you dare—"

"Don't get so excited. I wouldn't think of spreading such a story. You know me better than that. Anyway, I like the Macklins. I like them just as much as you do. I wouldn't for the world do them any harm!"

"All right. I'm sorry. But you remember, now!" Dinny said.

Trying to sound normal, Dinny added, "I have to run —things to do. Bye, now!" and took a little comfort in slamming the phone into its cradle as hard as she could.

Not until she was on her way to the bus did Dinny

think that she hadn't told Lissa the whole truth. "I didn't mean to lie," she thought. "I was just so *mad!* I don't know it's not glanders. And yet I told Lissa that nothing ailed the Lazy H horses but a cold in the head! I didn't say it on purpose—it just slipped out. Well, it can't be helped now."

The bus ride out to the ranch seemed to Dinny to take forever. She tried to pass the time by reading the signs along the way, signs she had seen many times before. But, as usual, she took no interest in being urged to use this tooth paste, buy that car, ask for the other cake mix. Finally, one sign—a new sign, Dinny realized—did kindle a spark of interest:

DON'T MISS OLD TIMERS' DAY AT CARNEY'S
LANDING—PARADE, SOFTBALL, CONTESTS,
PLENTY OF GOOD HOME STYLE FOOD—LOTS
OF FUN FOR YOUNG AND OLD!

Dinny smiled, remembering. Carney's Landing was a small town a few miles beyond the turn-off to the Lazy H. A couple of years ago she and her father had gone to Old Timers' Day, and it had been lots of fun. Maybe this year, if everything was all right by that time, she and Daddy and the Macklins could all go.

A few moments later Dinny got off the bus and walked to the Lazy H, her mind already too full of what was happening there to think any more about Old Timers' Day. When she reached the ranch, she found Janet alone in the kitchen, washing dishes. "Any news?" she asked, picking up a towel to dry the silver.

Janet shook her head. "No, nothing. Mom's upstairs with Dad, and I guess Mike's out tending the horses. Both Dr. Rudolph and Dr. Hanson have been here, but neither one of them would say anything. Just wait and see and don't worry." She scrubbed at a spot on a glass. "I *hate* being told not to worry when you would have to be soft in the head *not* to worry! Oh, Dinny, I'm so scared!"

Dinny was just about to say, "Don't worry," but she caught herself in time. Instead, she told the truth. "So am I. Jan, I'm scared to death! It's the waiting that is so awful. If only something would happen!"

"Don't say that," Janet begged. "If something does happen it's sure to be something bad."

The girls finished the dishes in silence. Then Janet said, "Would you put the things away, Dinny? I want to run upstairs and see Dad."

"Sure. When I'm done, I'll go out to the stall house and give Mike a hand."

Jan disappeared up the stairs. In a few moments Dinny had put the dishes into the cupboard. As she started for the door, the telephone rang.

She let it ring twice more. None of the family came to answer, so she went to the phone. "Lazy H Ranch."

She saw, out of the corner of her eye, that Jan and Mrs. Mac had come downstairs.

74

"Just a moment, please. Dr. Hanson calling," a woman's voice said.

Dinny held out the phone to Mrs. Mac. "It's the doctor. Do you want to—?"

Mrs. Mac's face was pure white. "I—I can't. I—no, you talk to him, Dinny."

"This is Diane Stoner," Dinny told the doctor. "Is there—is there any news?"

"Oh, hello, Dinny. Yes, there is some news. The report came in just now. Very fast service."

There was absolute silence in the kitchen behind Dinny. She turned to look at Mrs. Mac and Jan and saw that Mike was standing in the outside doorway. She swallowed hard.

"Wh—what does it say?" she asked.

CHAPTER 7

A Wonderful Idea

When Dinny turned away from the phone, her eyes lighted first on Mike. "Go take that sign down," she told him, her voice bubbling. "The Lazy H is back in business!"

"It's—it's all right?"

"*All* all right. Nothing but a simple little sickness. No glanders. Nothing catching. Isn't that wonderful?"

Mike gave her his biggest and best grin. "Taking that sign down will be the best thing I do all day!"

Mrs. Mac reached for a chair and lowered herself into it. "I am so relieved, I can't tell you! Jan, go tell your father—my legs will never make it all the way upstairs again right at the moment!"

The news acted as a tonic to Mr. Mac—so much so that

he came downstairs, bundled in a robe, to sit on the side porch for a while. "It's not that I feel so much better," he explained. "Only whatever I have, as long as it's not glanders, I am not going to baby it."

"So now you will probably catch something worse and be really sick," Mrs. Mac protested.

Her husband gave her a cheerful smile. "Well, if I do, I promise not to give it to the horses!"

Later in the morning, after she had helped Mike in the stall house, Dinny saddled Dreamdust and went for a long ride up into the hills.

On her way back to the ranch, she stopped in the little open spot in the trees. Leaving Dreamdust to enjoy the fine, soft grass, Dinny threw herself down at the edge of the stream.

She lay there quietly, thinking about the last few days. It seemed to be true that Mr. Mac had more than his share of bad luck. "Of course," Dinny said to herself, "it did turn out that the horses did not have glanders, but the scare was enough to shake the Macklins' spirit. Poor Mr. Mac. I can't bear to think that he might have to give up the ranch. If only there was something we could do to let everyone know about the Lazy H."

And then, all at once, Dinny's eyes opened wide and she sat up straight. "Oh!" she said out loud. "Oh, why didn't I think of that before?"

Startled by Dinny's voice, Dreamdust came over to see

what was the matter. Dinny jumped to her feet and gathered up the mare's lines. "Dreamy, old girl, I have just had an idea. A wonderful idea. Let's get back to the Lazy H fast!"

Dinny rode hard most of the way back, but in sight of the ranch she slowed Dreamdust to a walk. She was having second thoughts.

"Maybe I'm crazy," she told the little mare. "Maybe it's not such a wonderful idea after all." Then, "Yes, it is! I know it is! But suppose it doesn't work out? That would be just one more blow for Mr. Mac, and I'm not sure he can stand even one more. Maybe I had better just forget it."

Dinny rode into the stable yard, took the saddle off Dreamdust and gave her water. "If Mr. Mac is still on the porch," she decided, "I will take that as a sign that I should tell him."

The porch was empty. "Well," Dinny told herself, "that ends that!"

She was about to go into the house for a cool drink when Mike appeared out of the barn. "Good ride?"

"Yes, fine." Mike! Why hadn't she thought of Mike before? She would tell Mike about her idea. He could decide whether or not to tell Mr. Mac. "Mike, I want to talk to you. Come back to the barn for a minute."

"Well, what's the big hush-hush deal?" Mike asked, as they entered the barn. "Are we going to rob a bank, or what?" His face grew dark. "We'll probably *have* to rob a bank. There wasn't even a smell of a customer all the time you were gone."

"That's what I want to talk to you about, Mike. You know how your father always says that if he could only get people to know the Lazy H his problems would be solved?"

"Sure. Well, go on—don't keep me waiting."

"I've had an idea. I have thought of a really great way to get the Lazy H known—and all for free! Not only free, but lots of fun."

"You, girl, are crazy. But never let it be said that I'm not polite. I'll listen."

"Well, on the bus this morning I saw a big sign for Old Timers' Day at Carney's Landing." She told him about Old Timers' Day, what big crowds it drew from miles around, how much everyone enjoyed it.

"There is something going on all day, and at night there's square dancing. But what starts the day off is a big parade in the morning. Everybody's in it. There are two or three bands that march and all the clubs and organizations have big floats—do you follow me, Mike?"

Mike shook his head. "So Carney's Landing is having a big affair. Well, good for them. Sure, it sounds like a barrel of fun. Maybe we'll all go. But—"

"We won't just *go*. We'll be *part* of it. Mike, why can't we ride in the parade? A whole lot of us, riding Lazy H horses, with Lazy H signs on our backs! Can you think of a better way to make ourselves known?"

Light dawned in Mike's eyes, and he gave Dinny such a look of such admiration her heart bounced like a ball.

"Whatever you have in that head of yours, Dinny, you certainly know how to use it! That is a great scheme, the first bright one around here in ages. Listen, how do we go about getting into this parade?"

For the first time, Dinny's excitement slowed a little. "I don't know. But it wouldn't hurt to try, would it? Everybody else gets in. Mike, you do think it's worth telling your father about, don't you?"

Mike was silent, thinking it over. Then he shook his head. "No, I don't think we should tell Dad. Now wait a minute—don't look at me as if I had just taken your lollypop. Here is what I *do* think. I think you and I, as a committee from the Lazy H, should go to Carney's Landing and see what's what. If they tell us it's all right, we'll come home and spring it on Dad. He'll be crazy for it. But if they tell us to get lost, we won't mention it. Right?"

"Right! Oh, Mike—if only we can do it!"

He gave her a big grin. "Now listen. Right after lunch I'll tell Dad that you have an errand to do over in Carney's Landing—that's the truth; I won't be lying to him—and I'll ask if I can borrow the car and drive you over."

"Suppose he says no?"

"For a girl who has good ideas, you can throw more cold water on them afterwards than anybody I ever saw! Why should he say no? Now listen, don't go into the house grinning from ear to ear, or everybody is going to know something is up. And not a word to anyone!"

Lunch, although it was just sandwiches and milk, seemed to take as long as a formal dinner. Finally it was over. Mr. Mac leaned back in his chair and began to pack his pipe. "Wonder if there will be any riders this afternoon?" His voice was gloomy.

"There will be plenty tomorrow," Dinny said. "After all, the sign that said we were closed just came down a little while ago. There hasn't been time for many people to notice, yet. But by tomorrow . . ."

Relief showed in Mr. Mac's eyes. "Why, sure. That never crossed my mind," Mr. Mac said with a smile. "No wonder the place is empty."

Mike, deciding this was the right moment, told his father that Dinny had an errand to do in Carney's Landing. "Can I drive her over, Dad?" he asked.

"Of course," Mr. Mac said. "Likely we will be too busy tomorrow for you both to be gone at once."

On the drive to Carney's Landing, Mike and Dinny talked about school. Dinny was sorry to hear that Mike was still looking forward to returning to Locust Valley for his senior year. "Unless Dad's health improves, I would certainly hate to leave him alone with so much heavy work.

But he's set on my going and so is Mom, and—well, I want to go, myself."

"Jan will go to Springfield High, won't she?"

"Oh, sure. At first she didn't like the idea very much. But now that she has you to show her the ropes, she's all for it. She was telling me—"

"Wait," Dinny interrupted. "You turn left up here." When Mike had done so, and driven perhaps another half mile, Dinny told him, "There it is, spread out before you, though not as far as the eye can reach. That is Carney's Landing."

Mike slowed the car. "I'm glad you told me. I could have driven right on through without noticing." His eyes were merry. "Boy, is it ever small. And sleepy. But it's kind of cute, at that."

"Wait till you see it on Old Timers' Day—it isn't one bit sleepy then. Mike, look at the beards."

Sure enough, practically every man on the street had some kind of growth of hair on his chin, some rich and full, some thin. Mike didn't understand, until Dinny spotted the sign, NO SHAVES UNTIL AFTER OLD TIMERS' DAY. "When Dad and I were here the other time all the men wore beards," Dinny explained. "If you don't grow a beard, you have to pay a fine."

There was another sign, a big one, on a banner hanging across Main Street between the fire house and Bisby's Grocery store, which read, MAKE THIS THE BEST

AND BIGGEST OLD TIMERS' DAY EVER! Under-
neath were listed some of the events that would take place
on the biggest day ever, and below, in smaller letters, ANY-
ONE WISHING TO ENTER THE PARADE, REGISTER WITH THE
CHAMBER OF COMMERCE.

"That answers the first question," Mike said, as he
parked the car. "Now the next thing, where do they keep
their Chamber of Commerce?"

They walked up one side of Main Street—all eight
blocks of it—and down the other, without finding the
office. Finally Mike went up to an old man, one of those
with a bushy beard, who was sunning himself on a bench
in front of the Railroad Hotel. "Excuse me. Can you tell
me where I can find the Chamber of Commerce?"

The old man smiled. "Sure thing." He pointed down
the street. "Meets up above Bisby's store."

"Thank you very much," Mike said, and started off.

"Wait up, boy. You won't find them now. Chamber
meets second Tuesday of the month, eight o'clock sharp."

Dinny decided it was time for her to take a hand.
Giving the old man her nicest smile she said, "Well,
maybe you can help us. We want to find out about the
Old Timers' Day parade."

The old man thought it over. "George Bisby's your
best bet, I should judge. He's president of the Chamber.
Find him in his store."

"Fine. Thanks a lot."

"Or if he is not in the store, likely he will be in Tom's shop getting a haircut. Seems to me he remarked just this morning he needed one."

"Oh. Well, we'll find him."

"If he is not in the barber's, try the Soda Shop. Gets him one of those sundaes every afternoon along about this time. Great sweet tooth, George has."

Dinny threw Mike a look that cut off his laughter. "We can find him. Thank you ever so much." Then she rushed Mike away before his laughter got the better of his manners.

They found Mr. Bisby in his store. Once more, Mike took over. "Mr. Bisby? My name is Mike Macklin, and this is Dinny Stoner. We want to find out about the Old Timers' Day parade. Can you help us?"

He gave them a cheery smile. "Well, maybe I can,

maybe I can't. Happens the chairman of the parade committee is out of town. What was it you wanted to know?"

"We want to be in the parade," Mike told him.

"You two?" He looked from one to the other.

Dinny brought out her smile again. "Oh, not just us. You see, Mr. Bisby, Mike's father owns the Lazy H Ranch. It's a riding stable. We thought we could bring over the Lazy H horses and ride in the parade."

Mr. Bisby scratched his head. "Well, I don't know . . ."

"They are beautiful horses," Dinny went on. "Western horses, you know—paint ponies and a gray and a strawberry roan, and a lot more. And we are all good riders, so you don't have to worry about that. We wear Western riding clothes—cowboy boots and jeans and bright shirts and all." She drew a long breath. "It would be very gay. I think people would love to see us. Mr. Mac's horse, Prince, does all sorts of tricks, and Dreamdust, the one I ride, can—"

Mr. Bisby put up his hand. "Now wait a minute, wait a minute! If I had the say I'd tell you yes right on the spot, you're such a good salesman. As I said, the parade chairman's out of town, or I would take you to see him right now and settle it." He reached under the counter, brought out pencil and paper and gave them to Mike. "Tell you what, you write down the name and address of the place. Next time the committee meets, I will take it up and let you know one way or the other. How's that?"

"That will be fine, and thank you very much." But Dinny wished that they could get it settled now, so they could go back and tell Mr. Mac this very day. She knew how much it would mean to him.

Some of her disappointment must have shown in her voice, for Mr. Bisby told her, "Now, don't you worry. I will make out a real good case for you. Let you in on a little secret, too. Parade chairman's a bug on horses. Most likely he'll jump at the idea."

"Oh, thanks so much! I'm sure you *will* do your best for us." Dinny beamed at him. "And you won't be sorry. We will add an extra something to the parade; just you wait and see if we don't!"

Mike thanked Mr. Bisby, too, and gave him the paper on which he had written the name and address of the Lazy H. He and Dinny started out of the store.

At the door, Dinny had a sudden thought. She turned back. "Mr. Bisby? Who is the parade chairman, anyway?"

"Why, Mr. Winslow. Mr. Homer Winslow."

"Oh," said Dinny. "Oh." And she made a dash for the street, with Mike close behind.

As they started for the car, Mike told her, "You were just great. You really laid it on. You could charm the birds out of the trees, Dinny. If you ask me, the parade is in the bag."

But not even Mike's compliments could cheer Dinny. "Oh no, it isn't. We don't even have a chance."

Mike stopped in his tracks. "You're crazy. What makes you say that?"

"Didn't you hear? Mr. Winslow is the parade chairman."

"So?" Mike frowned. "What are you getting at?"

"Mr. *Winslow*. Bud Winslow's father, silly! Bud is the boy I told to get off the Lazy H and never come back!"

CHAPTER 8

Activity at the Lazy H

It was Sunday evening. Almost a week had gone by, and there had been no word from the Old Timers' Day people.

"With Bud's father as chairman of the committee," Dinny thought, "we have about as much chance of getting into that parade as I have of being elected President of the United States. And, as usual, it's my fault. If I just hadn't flown off the handle at Bud that day!"

Business all week at the Lazy H had been about as bad as it could be. They had no more than two or three riders a day. Even on Friday, the twelve-girl riding club had gone down to seven. Suddenly Dinny saw Lissa in her mind's eye. "If I thought for one minute that Lissa Lambert had been spreading that nasty talk about the sickness at the Lazy H, I'd—oh, I don't know what I would do. Tell Mike on her, I guess. That would fix her. Mike may be a little soft in the head when it comes to Lissa, but he wouldn't stand for that."

Better go to bed, Dinny decided. That was the simplest way to get tomorrow here in a hurry. Perhaps then there would be good news. Perhaps, even, a "Yes" from the parade committee, though that seemed too much to hope for.

Dinny lay a long time staring at the dark ceiling, trying to spark another—maybe even a better—idea to help out the Macklins. But none came. Finally she drifted off, to dream about a big parade in which dozens of horses marched in stiff rows.

When she woke, Dinny had a feeling it was later than usual. Looking at the clock on her night table, she could hardly believe what she saw. Twenty-five minutes after nine? Why, it couldn't be! What about Daddy's breakfast? What about—? She leaped out of bed, slid her arms into her robe, and went sailing down the stairs.

There was a note propped against the sugar bowl on the kitchen table. "You slept right through the alarm," it said, "and you looked so tired I didn't have the heart to wake you. See you tonight . . . Dad"

From that bad start, it went right on being one of those nothing-right mornings. Dinny burned her toast, broke a cup, pulled a button off her shirt getting dressed. The phone rang twice—once the wrong number and once a man wanting to sell her a set of books. Then Mrs. Cash, from next door, came to borrow two eggs and stayed to chat about nothing. That made Dinny miss the eleven o'clock bus, so she had to wait half an hour. It was after twelve before she arrived at the Lazy H.

There she found things as bad as they had been at home. Two women and a little boy were waiting. At the fence, Janet—practically in tears—was trying once again to saddle Winky, the pony, as she had her first day at the ranch, and was making no better progress.

Seeing Dinny, Janet greeted her with a wail. "They haven't any right to go away and leave me to handle everything!" She dropped Winky's saddle to the ground. "I hate this place! I hate horses!"

"Don't throw a fit in front of customers!" Dinny ordered. She picked up the saddle, told Winky sharply, "Get over there!" Crowding him to the fence, she dropped the saddle on his back. "See? I've told you over and over, Janet. You have to let horses know you are boss. Where is everybody?"

"Dad's out with a riding party," Janet told her. "Mom cut her arm, Mike drove her to the doctor, and . . ."

Dinny's temper snapped. "And you're a total loss by yourself! Why don't you go have a good cry, and let me handle this?"

Tossing her head, Janet marched into the house. Dinny

came up with a smile for the two waiting women. "Things seem to be a little mixed up this morning," she said. "I'll have your horses ready in a minute."

"Things always seem to be mixed up around here," one of the women answered sharply.

"Hold your tongue," Dinny told herself, as she rushed into the stall house. "Remember, the customer is always right!" She saddled Comanche and Apache in record time and led them out to the yard.

As the two women mounted, one said to the other, "I think these spotted horses are so ugly, don't you?"

Dinny swallowed the not very polite comment that rose to her lips, helped the little boy up on Winky, and gave a sigh of relief as the three riders left the yard and started up the trail.

"I suppose," she thought, "I ought to go find Jan." And then, "No, there's work to do first."

Shortly after that, Mr. Mac and his party returned. He looked very tired. "Mike and Mrs. Mac back yet?"

Dinny shook her head. "Not yet. Look, I'll take the horses. Why don't you go get yourself a cup of coffee."

With a faint smile, he disappeared into the house. A moment later, the station wagon pulled in. Dinny ran over. "Are you all right, Mrs. Mac?"

"Oh, I'm fine. It was nothing." But her face was drained of color.

"Oh, sure, a mere nothing," Mike put in. "The doctor

had to take five stitches, but it was nothing. Come on, Mom, you had better lie down a while." He took his mother inside, while Dinny returned to the stall house.

It wasn't long before Mike came back. "What's the matter with Jan?" he demanded. "She's been crying."

Dinny had managed to get a grip on her temper, but now, at Mike's accusing tone, it slipped again. "I called her a big baby—and she is! Scared to death! She had the whole place mixed up the minute she was left alone."

"Well, for Pete's sake, she can't help it. Being afraid of horses is no crime. Lots of people are. The trouble with you, Dinny, is that you believe your way of thinking is the only right way!" Then he saw a stall standing empty. "Hey, where's Winky?"

"On trail!" Dinny snapped. "The little Julian boy is riding him."

"Alone?"

"Oh, for goodness sakes, of course not! His mother and his aunt are with him."

"Why didn't you go along?"

"Because I didn't dare leave Jan alone here, that's why!" Dinny slammed her hand against the wall. "Now look here, Mike Macklin! What do you think I am, anyway? Twins? If you don't like the way I do things, maybe you had better find someone else!"

"Someone who will get paid for being a stable boy,"

92

Mike said. "Why don't you say that, too, as long as you're getting your complaints off your chest?"

For a moment they stood almost toe to toe, glaring at each other. "If I were a boy he would punch me," Dinny thought. Then Mike turned on his heels, grabbed the broom and went to work cleaning out the stalls.

Dinny left the stall house, certain that if she stayed near Mike one of them would start the fight all over again. By now, Jan had probably told her parents the mean way Dinny had treated her. "Maybe I should just go home," she thought. She could take a ride, but that would mean going back to the stall house, where Mike was, to get Dreamdust. Slowly she started up the road that led away from the ranch.

She reached the point where that road joined the larger one, and without thinking she opened the mail box. There was one letter. The return address was *Carney's Landing Old Timers' Day Committee.*

For a second, Dinny's heart leaped. Then she reminded herself that Mr. Bisby had said he would let them know "one way or the other."

"This," Dinny thought sadly, "is no doubt the *other*— the 'No' which is the only answer we can expect. Well, I can just open it to make sure and then throw it away and forget the whole business!"

But then her eyes went to the address on the envelope, and she saw with dismay that the letter was directed to

Mr. Hubert Macklin. Why, neither she nor Mike could open it. You can't open a letter addressed to someone else! Now Mr. Mac would know all about it—and add one more disappointment to a list already too long!

"This," Dinny thought, "puts the finishing touch on a miserable day!" Tucking the letter into her pocket, she began to walk slowly back to the Lazy H.

When she reached the stable yard, Dinny saw trouble. The little Julian boy was on the porch with Mrs. Mac and his aunt bending over him, while his mother stood at the foot of the porch steps having an argument with Mr. Mac. Jan and Mike were just standing there, looking helpless.

Seeing Dinny—and forgetting their quarrel—Jan rushed over. "Did you ever? Timmy Julian asked to go barefoot and his mother *let* him. The first thing he did was step on a nail, and now his mother is giving *Dad* a bad time. To hear her, you would think Dad had *hammered* the nail in Timmy's foot!"

At that point Mr. Mac's voice rose. "Worried? Of course I'm worried. I'm worried about Timmy's foot— and I'm also worried, if you don't mind my saying so, about any mother who lets her child run barefoot around a stable! Let's not stand here arguing. Take Timmy to a doctor and get him a shot. I don't admit that I am responsible, but I will pay the bill."

Timmy's mother and aunt bundled him into the car and

drove away. Watching them go, Mr. Mac shook his head slowly. "It's just one thing after another! That's about the last straw. I don't think I can take any more."

Dinny had been standing there with half her attention on the Julians, half on trying to figure out a way to break the bad news she carried in her pocket. Now, deciding there was no easy way, she took the letter out, thrust it toward Mr. Mac and said, "That may not be the last straw, but I'm afraid this is!"

They all stared at her. Mr. Mac, expecting disaster, said, "From the look on your face, I had better take this sitting down. Let's all go up on the porch."

It seemed to Dinny that Mr. Mac took forever and then some to read the letter. First he glanced through it, then went back and read more slowly. At last he raised his eyes—and began to laugh!

"What is it?" Mrs. Mac wanted to know.

"It's from the Old Timers' Day Committee of Carney's Landing. Listen, I'll read it to you.

"*Dear Mr. Macklin: We take pleasure in informing you that your application to enter the Lazy H Ranch in the Old Timers' Day Parade has been approved. Upon payment of a five-dollar entrance fee we will send you your parade permit and number in the line. We are looking forward to having you with us.* The letter is signed *George Bisby, Chairman.*" Mr. Mac looked up, his eyes twinkling.

"Now wait, that's not all. There is something written across the bottom. It says, *P.S. Please tell Miss Dinny that Mr. Winslow says he is willing to forgive and forget as he knows his son can be a pain in the neck sometimes.* All right, Dinny, my girl—just what is this all about?"

But Dinny was too excited to get out three sensible words in a row—and the others were too excited to listen if she had. Janet and Mrs. Mac kept asking each other, "What does it mean? What is it all about?" but neither one waited for a reply. Mr. Mac smiled at the letter in his lap, and once he patted it, for all the world as if it were alive. Mike beamed at Dinny as though he had invented her, and kept asking the world at large, "Isn't she great?"

As for Dinny herself, she had never, never been this happy before. For once, something was working out! And —and oh, the look in Mike's eyes! That look was for *her!*

Seeing everyone calm down a little, Mike began to explain. He told about their visit to Carney's Landing, and gave full credit to Dinny for having the idea in the first place and for doing an excellent job of selling.

"Won't it be swell, Dad?" he concluded. "Talk about promoting the Lazy H!"

They all agreed it was about the best ever. "We will have to make plans," Mrs. Mac reminded them. "Who is going to ride which horse, what we will wear, and all. Dinny on Dreamdust, of course, and you, Hub, on

Prince." She laughed, sounding like a girl. "I guess I'll ride Mousie. Her gray matches all the gray hairs I have acquired since we took over the Lazy H!"

Mr. Mac looked at her with surprise. "You?"

"Why not? We want to look as good as possible, don't we? We can't let people think the Lazy H has only a few horses, for heaven's sake."

"I'll take Apache," Mike put in, "and you take Comanche, Sis. That way we can ride the two paint ponies side by side. They even keep step."

Janet didn't answer him for a while. "I would rather ride Little Sister," she finally said in a small voice—to her father, not to Mike.

She did not get the help she expected. Mr. Mac sounded pleasant but firm. "Little Sister will stay right home," he said. "I don't want to have to stop half the way through the parade and carry that lazy nag the rest of the route!"

"We really should round up some more riders," Mrs. Mac said quickly, heading off an argument. "At least two, anyway, to ride Kewpie and Comet."

"How about Mr. and Mrs. Pace?" Dinny suggested. "They usually ride those two, anyway, and besides they are much the nicest of the regular customers. Anyway—"

"Anyway," Mike finished for her, "they have little Billy, and he could ride Winky, and that would give all the mothers at the parade the idea of going riding and bringing their children along—right, Dinny?"

"That's what I had in mind," she admitted. To herself, she added, "And I'm glad you and I are back on speaking terms, Mike."

"What are we going to wear?" Jan asked. "Signs or something, I mean. There is no sense riding in the parade if we don't let people know we are from the Lazy H."

Mrs. Mac solved that problem. Signs painted on paper, she pointed out, were likely to get torn and would be hard to fasten on, besides. She would get some sturdy cloth in bright colors, cut it to size, and stitch LAZY H RANCH—ROCK RIDGE ROAD on a piece for each rider.

"Well, that seems to cover everything for now," Mr. Mac decided. "Shall we close the meeting and get something done? Mike, suppose you drive in to Carney's Landing and pay our entrance fee, before they change their minds. Take your mother along and she can pick up material for the signs. I'll ride Prince over to the Paces and ask them. All right to leave you two girls in charge here?"

Dinny and Janet looked at each other, and then began to laugh. "Of course," Dinny said.

"Sure, it is," Janet agreed.

Mr. Mac stood up. "Well, let's get rolling. You know, if things will just go smoothly for us between now and the parade, this may be the salvation of the Lazy H."

For the next two weeks nothing very serious happened. In fact, as Dinny said several times—crossing her fingers

—everything was calm, almost too calm. Little by little they got ready for the parade, saddle soaping and polishing the saddles and shining the metal work on them, cleaning saddle blankets, having the traveling blacksmith put new shoes on the horses who needed them. The Paces had eagerly agreed to form a part of the Lazy H parade group—in fact, little Billy Pace became something of a pest, turning up at all hours to ask if it was time for the parade and having to be taken home to his worried mother. Each time he promised never to run away again—and next day he would be back.

Dinny's father had offered his services. Mr. Mac tried

to persuade him to ride, but he drew the line there. However, he would drive the station wagon which would carry spare gear and extra saddles in case of need. "And I'll cheer for you," he told them, grinning. "I'll be right in the front row, leading the cheering section."

"It has to be nice weather. It just *has* to be!" If Dinny said that once, she said it a hundred times. And when, finally, the big day dawned, she had her wish. The weather was perfect.

Dinny and her father stayed at the ranch the night before.

By five-thirty in the morning the Paces had arrived, making a very handsome group in new, scarlet shirts.

"Billy's so excited, I don't think he slept a wink," Mrs. Pace said. Then, with a smile, "I might as well admit that his father and I didn't do much better!"

Of course the Lazy H money could not run to such a luxury as a horse van. Each horse was to be ridden over to Carney's Landing, arriving in plenty of time to be rubbed down, watered and rested before the parade.

Mike and Mr. Mac saddled for the Paces. A rope was put around Winky's neck so he could be led over to Carney's Landing. The long ride would be too much for Billy, and he was to come over in the station wagon with Dinny's father.

Dinny offered to help Mrs. Mac saddle, but she said she was making out fine, so Dinny went along the runway to see how Janet was doing. She found Comanche, still bare of back, standing alone in his stall, and Jan nowhere in sight. For a moment Dinny could not imagine where she might be, and then an idea struck her. Going down to Little Sister's stall, she found Janet trying to put the big saddle up on the old mare's sway back.

"What are you doing?" Dinny demanded, as if it were not perfectly obvious.

"Saddling Little Sister. I'm going to ride her."

By then Mike had noticed what was going on. He came along and stood listening. Then he asked. "Why, Sis?"

"Because I'm scared of Comanche, that's why. Well, not really scared, but—but not comfortable. Dad will let me ride Little Sister if I tell him that this parade isn't going to be one bit of fun for me if I ride Comanche!"

Dinny drew a long breath. She knew that if she lost her temper that would only make Janet all the more determined to ride Little Sister. Anyway, it would be a shame to spoil their wonderful day by starting it with a fight. So she said, in a careful voice, "But Jan, that's not why we are riding in this parade, remember? Not for fun, I mean. We are riding in it to attract a lot of new customers to the Lazy H so—so your father won't lose all his money! Little Sister won't help the stable, believe me. She looks as if she ought to be pulling a junk wagon. She will scare customers away."

"Oh . . ." Janet's expression changed. "I didn't think of it that way."

"There! For once I didn't fly off the handle!" Dinny told herself. But she hadn't counted on Mike, who couldn't leave well enough alone. "Din, you shouldn't make Jan ride Comanche if she doesn't want to."

Dinny looked at him. "I'm not *making* her ride Comanche, for Pete's sake. I'm just saying that Little Sister will spoil the whole show. It would be better for Jan not to ride at all than to ride Little Sister—that's all I'm saying!"

"Well, you have a point there," Mike agreed.

Janet's face showed plainly what she thought of the idea of not riding at all. She appealed to her brother. "Mike, can I handle Comanche in the parade?"

He considered. "You can if you believe you can. You have ridden him often enough. Comanche is perfectly safe—"

Janet cut him short. "All right, I'll ride Comanche! Let's not *talk* about it any more. Let's just *go!*"

Dinny felt she ought to say something more to Jan, but for the life of her she could not think of anything that would sound encouraging. So she let it go, and went to saddle Dreamdust.

A few minutes later the riders started out, leaving Dinny's father and Billy Pace at the gate, waving goodby. "See you later," they called.

The riders moved slowly in order not to make the horses

too hot. As they went, Dinny kept reaching out every few moments to stroke the little mare's neck. Once she told her, "We're going to have fun, you and I. Why, Dreamy, I'll bet you will be the star of the show!"

"It's going to be a wonderful day," she thought, enjoying the warmth of the sun on her back, listening to the horses' hoof beats. "A wonderful day. Cross your fingers, Dinny!" But what for? What could go wrong now?

"No, I don't have to cross my fingers. Nothing can spoil today—nothing, nothing, nothing!"

CHAPTER 9

Here Comes the Parade

When the Lazy H group reached Carney's Landing, they found Dinny's father and Billy waiting for them. Mr. Stoner had made arrangements for the horses to be tied up in a lot near the parade's starting line.

"We have plenty of time," Dinny said, after the horses had been watered and groomed. "Why don't we take a walk and see the sights?"

"A good idea," Mike said. "We'll all go."

"I'll stay here and keep away any small boys with sling shots," Mr. Stoner said. "All of you go ahead and have a good time."

Dinny walked down Main Street with Mike. The town, with banners draped across the streets, looked very gay. Even though it was still early, there was a huge crowd.

"Wait till tonight," Dinny said, "when the lights are all on and the band is playing. It will really be something. Look—see that street that is blocked off? That's where there will be dancing tonight."

"We'll dance our legs off up to the knees." Mike said it so easily that it was a moment before Dinny realized what he had said.

"Why, he's asked me for a date!" she thought. "Well, anyway, sort of a date. Or sort of asked me. Oh, Mike!"

They turned back toward the lot where the horses were tied. When they got there, Mr. Bisby was rushing about trying to get the floats lined up in the right order. Besides being chairman of the affair, he was also Grand Marshal of the parade.

Finally, the parade was ready to start. The Lazy H riders mounted and watched the first part start out, while they eagerly waited their turn to join the line. The high school band led off, followed by a number of floats— Boy Scouts, Girl Scouts, business firms, service clubs— some of them very fancy.

The Lazy H had drawn position number sixteen. Just ahead of them was the float of the Carney's Landing Dairy, which consisted of a truck with a large Guernsey cow tied firmly on top of it. Beside the cow stood a pretty girl in a blue cotton dress with sun bonnet to match. Just before the float moved, a man lifted the girl onto the cow's back.

Mike laughed. "She's going to have a tougher ride than any of us. Cows have more bones than anyone has a right to, and they wear them all in their backs. Say, that's our signal! Up and at them, Lazy H!"

Mr. Mac, riding Prince, led the Lazy H group. Janet and Mike followed on the two paints. Dinny rode in the middle. Then came the Pace family. Mrs. Mac brought up the rear on Mousie.

They were a big hit. Dinny was thrilled by the cheers that greeted them. She smiled at the crowds that lined the streets. Up ahead, Prince, the big show-off, was really enjoying himself, holding his head and picking up his feet in a manner that would have done credit to a

race horse. He stepped to the side and back and generally behaved, as Dinny thought with affection, like the big ham he was.

Following more slowly, Apache and Comanche kept step perfectly, as if parades were their favorite form of pleasure. Dreamdust was at her best, picking her way carefully along, ears pricked, neck arched, tail like a banner. Every block or so Dinny would lean forward a little in the saddle and signal with a touch of her toe. The little mare would neigh, rear up on her hind legs, turn a dancing circle and come down again in what looked for all the world like a bow to the audience.

At the conclusion of one of those tricks, Dinny saw her

father watching her with shining pride on his face, and she felt as if she had been given a beautiful, expensive present. She knew what the gift was, too: understanding. She and her father understood each other now. *Liked* each other, which is sometimes more important—and harder to achieve—than loving each other!

Coming back from that moment of thought, Dinny realized that they were near the end of the parade route at the foot of Main Street. Here the marchers turned into a field that was already filling up with people. Dinny saw the Rainbow Girls' drill team turn off, then a large float covered with purple crepe paper flowers, then the dairy maid—*she* was probably thankful it was over, Dinny thought with a grin. Next it was the Lazy H riders' turn. Mr. Mac shot a quick glance over his shoulder to check on his party and pulled Prince to the left.

Then it happened.

A little boy in a cowboy suit dashed out from the curb, paying no attention to his mother's grasping hand, or her cry of "Come back here!" For all the world like the villain in a TV Western, he planted himself in front of Comanche, so that Janet had to pull the horse up sharply to avoid running him down.

"Reach!" yelled the little boy, waving a big Colt .45 cap pistol. Comanche edged away. Janet screamed.

"Reach!" cried the boy again. And then he fired his gun directly into Comanche's lowered face.

The horse gathered his big, powerful body together. Janet screamed again, a shrill, high, "No, no, no!"

Mike made a wild grab for Comanche's reins—and missed. With a scream of rage and fright, Comanche bolted.

There was an instant of time in which there seemed to be no sound but the fading beat of Comanche's hoofs. Then together, as the crowd began to shout and mill around, Mr. Mac and Mike drove their heels into their horses' sides and took off in pursuit. Dinny heeled Dreamdust and followed.

Prince, big and powerful, drew ahead almost at once. Behind him, Apache followed and then the smaller, slower Dreamdust. As Dinny rode, she felt terror growing in her until she could feel it, stinging, in her eyes, taste it, bitter, in her mouth. She heard the drumming of other hoofs, then a sobbing sound which she did not realize, until she began to choke, was coming from her own throat. Up ahead, Mr. Mac disappeared over a small rise.

After Dreamdust topped the rise, she floundered to a quick stop. Mr. Mac was already off his horse. Mike was sliding out of his saddle. Dinny saw Mr. Mac drop to his knees beside something on the ground. Something that lay very still.

It took Dinny a moment to realize that the something was Janet. Janet, who lay without moving, like a heap of old clothes. Like a heap of clothes with no one inside.

CHAPTER 10

The Dreamdust Fund

Without remembering that she had jumped off Dreamdust, Dinny found herself on the ground. She tried to move, but her feet refused to take a step. She could only stand there, clinging to Dreamdust's saddle, feeling as if she were in the middle of a bad dream.

Soon an ambulance roared up, and two men in white coats jumped out and ran to Mr. Mac and Mike beside Janet. Then a car came, out of which a man rushed. "I'm a doctor!" he called. Then more cars drove up. A stranger helped Mrs. Mac out of one of them and over to the little group. Still more cars, more people crowding around, the clacking sound of many voices asking questions to which no one knew the answers.

Now Dinny could not see Janet at all. There were

110

too many legs, a forest of legs forming a block between her and the sad little heap that lay so still. Dinny felt as if her body had no blood or bones, her mind no thought but one word repeating itself over and over inside her head. *"Please! Please!"*

At last the two ambulance men very gently picked up Janet, who was wrapped in blankets. The doctor and Mrs. Mac got into the ambulance with Janet, and Mr. Mac joined the two men on the front seat. The ambulance moved away.

The people who had come out from town still milled around. Two figures drew away from the crowd. One came toward Dinny. She shook her head, trying to clear it. Mr. Pace was beside her. He gave her an anxious look. "Dinny, are you all right?"

"Yes. I'm all right." Her voice sounded odd, as if she hadn't spoken for years. She cleared her throat and tried again. "Jan? Is Janet—"

That was all she could get out, but Mr. Pace understood. "They don't know, Dinny. They can't tell, till they get her to the hospital. So . . ." His voice trailed away.

"Mike is taking Prince to see if he can find Comanche," Mr. Pace said after a moment. "I'll lead Apache back. I can lead Dreamdust, too—"

Dinny was beginning to feel better. "I'm all right. I can ride." Getting up her courage, she mounted and made herself sit straight in the saddle.

"Good girl!" Mr. Pace went off, but came back in a moment with Comet and Apache. Just as they were about to start off, Mike appeared on Prince, with Comanche walking calmly behind.

"Found him just over the hill," Mike explained, "eating his head off as if nothing had happened." Dinny saw in his face a tight, hard expression. When she tried to meet his eyes he refused to look at her.

In silence, they rode slowly back to where they had left the horses early this morning. As they passed, people stared and stepped back, making room for them. "As if," Dinny thought, "we were a funeral procession!"

Dinny's father and Mrs. Pace were waiting, with the station wagon packed and ready to go.

"Dinny, you ride in the car," her father suggested, but she refused. Winky had to be led, and Mrs. Pace wasn't a good enough rider to lead the pony.

The slow ride back to the Lazy H seemed endless. How different from this morning, Dinny thought, when they had all been so excited and happy, looking forward to the parade so eagerly. When at last they reached the ranch, the Paces led their horses to the stable and went home. Mike and Dinny and her father began to water and groom the horses. And to wait. Wait for news of Janet.

When the stable work was finished, there was nothing to do—nothing, at least, that they could make themselves do—but sit in the house in silence.

Mike's silence, Dinny realized after a while, was different from her own or her father's. "It is as if," she decided, "he doesn't like our being here. As if he is terribly angry, even more angry than worried." She wanted so much to say something to him, but she could think of nothing.

At last they heard the sound they were waiting for. A car pulled into the stable yard, then started away again. Someone had brought the Macklins home.

The three in the house rushed out to meet them. It was Mr. Stoner who asked, "How is she?"

"They can't be sure," Mrs. Mac replied. "No skull damage, which the doctor was afraid of. There are broken bones, and a—a back injury. But that's all they will say—that they cannot be sure, yet, what will happen."

That made Mike break his silence. "You mean—you mean Janet might be—be *crippled?*"

Mr. Mac dropped into a chair, hiding his gray face in his hands. His wife went to sit on the arm of the chair beside him, her hands on his shoulders. "They don't know, son. Not yet."

The anger that had been boiling in Mike burst out. He whirled to face Dinny. "It's your fault—it's all your fault! You made her ride Comanche!"

The words were like stones. Dinny could feel each one of them striking her, hurting her, and she moved toward her father. Her father's arm slipped around her. The dull feeling that had gripped her since the accident suddenly melted away.

"It *is* true!" she sobbed. "I did it—I made Janet ride Comanche!"

Mr. Mac was suddenly on his feet. "Be quiet, both of you! Listen to me!" The stern voice had its effect. Dinny and Mike turned to him.

"What happened was an accident," Mr. Mac went on. "Nobody could have prevented it. Janet was perfectly capable of riding Comanche under ordinary circumstances. If I hadn't known that, I would not have let her ride him. Dinny is not to blame. Nor is Janet, herself. Nor even the little boy with the cap pistol—he didn't know any better. What happened could have happened as easily to Prince or Apache or Dreamdust, and any one of those three would have bolted, too. A frightened horse running away is almost impossible for *any* rider to control."

He stopped and drew a long breath. "So I don't want to hear any more of this nonsense. What happened was *nobody's* fault. Understand, Mike?"

"Yes, sir," Mike said in a quiet voice.

"Dinny?"

"Yes, Mr. Mac."

Mr. Stoner's arm was tight around Dinny. "Come on, honey. We had better be getting home."

Dinny nodded. What she wanted most then was to get away from Mike's accusing eyes.

But even away from Mike, her thoughts just would not make sense. "I said *yes* to Mr. Mac," she thought, "but I can't say *yes* to myself! All I can say is, *if only.* If only I hadn't shamed Janet, telling her we were not riding in the parade for fun. If only she had stuck to her guns and ridden Little Sister. Or if only Mike had talked me down. No, it's not fair to try to shift the blame to Janet or to Mike. I was the one who got Jan to ride Comanche. Oh, if only I hadn't!"

After a night made up partly of terrible dreams, partly of long periods when she was wide awake, Dinny opened her eyes. It was daylight. She lay still, trying to decide what day this was. Yesterday, Old Timers' Day, had been Saturday. This must be Sunday. Between today and yesterday a thousand years seemed to have crawled by!

Her whole body felt heavy and tired. "This is how it feels to be old," she thought as she got up. A shower and the blue robe that was her father's favorite did not help a bit. Dinny still felt miserable. "At least," she told herself, "Daddy will be home today. I won't have to wait for news alone."

Waiting was very hard, though, alone or in company. Last night Mrs. Mac had promised she would call as soon as there was any news, but it was noon before she heard the phone ring.

Dinny heard Mrs. Mac's voice saying that Janet had a

broken collar bone and a broken leg, but what was thought a back injury proved to be only a bad bruise.

"She will have to stay in the hospital, of course," Mrs. Mac explained. "And there is always some danger the first few days. Mr. Mac and I are at the hospital now, and we want to be with her as much as possible." She hesitated. "I don't like to ask you, dear, after the way Mike acted last night, but do you suppose you could go out to the Lazy H? We have to keep the stables running, and Mike cannot handle everything by himself."

"Of course," Dinny promised. She was glad Mrs. Mac had asked her. She was anxious to do anything she could to help. But she remembered the look on Mike's face, and—oh, she dreaded meeting Mike there, alone!

It turned out to be every bit as bad as she feared. Mike plainly held to his belief that the accident had been Dinny's fault. And though Dinny had agreed and said so, that had not helped at all. Sunday afternoon and all of Monday passed in silence. When it was absolutely necessary to speak, Mike was polite but in a cold way. That was much harder for Dinny to stand than if Mike had yelled at her.

By Tuesday morning, Mike's silent treatment was becoming almost too much for Dinny. The only thing, Dinny felt, that kept her from flying apart at the seams was that the Lazy H was busy. But would it last? Most of those who came to ride, Dinny realized, did so out of curiosity.

Around noon, while Mike was out with a party, Mr. and Mrs. Mac came home, looking terribly tired but happy. Janet, they reported, was definitely out of the woods. Now the only thing necessary for her to be all well again was time.

"A long time, I am afraid," Mrs. Mac said, "but no matter. She will be fine—that is what counts."

Mr. Mac sighed. Dinny realized that behind his pleasure at Janet's good progress there was an anxious tone in his voice.

"How about some coffee?" he asked his wife. Then, to Dinny, "I have something to tell you. Let's go out on the porch."

"Janet's accident will mean a lot of bills, Dinny," Mr. Mac said when they were seated on the porch. "Doctor and hospital bills. And—well, there just isn't any money to pay them. Sure, business has improved at the stables, but that's not enough." He hesitated, shaking his head. "Of course, we have accident insurance. But the policy says riders are covered only while on the grounds of the Lazy H and on the trails we use. So—well, the insurance isn't going to be any help in Janet's case."

He was silent for so long that Dinny realized he was having trouble getting up courage for what he had to say next. She felt her heart begin to thud. What was wrong? What else *could* be wrong?

"I—Dinny, I hate to tell you this. But I know you will

117

understand. Now I will have to sell Prince and Dreamdust. I will have to accept Colonel Gill's offer."

Dinny sat very still, her heart pounding in her ears. "I won't cry," she told herself. "Not now. I won't let Mr. Mac see me cry." Then she said, in a strange voice that sounded as if it came from far away, "I—I'm not very surprised. Maybe I knew all along, somewhere inside me, that I just wasn't meant ever to own Dreamdust. Of course, you have to sell. I know you wouldn't if you could help it." She stood up, struggling to keep back the tears. "I—I guess I will go home now."

All the way down to the bus, her heart and her feet made of lead, Dinny kept her promise to herself not to cry. She kept it on the long bus ride, too, and on the walk home from the bus. She didn't cry until she was in her own room. Then she flung herself down on her bed and let the tears come in a flood until there were no more tears left to cry.

Turning over on her back, Dinny stared blankly at the ceiling, trying to make sense of her thoughts. "It was my fault that Janet got hurt. And now I am going to lose Dreamdust."

She got up and went to her dresser for a fresh handkerchief. There, under the pile of them, she saw an edge of blue. Her bank book. She pulled it out and opened it. "One hundred twenty dollars," she read out loud. "I

didn't add much to my Dreamdust Fund this summer.
But I have no use for the money now."

She sat down on the edge of the bed, still holding the
bank book. No use for the money? Yes, of course there
was a use for it. A *right* use. Oh, one hundred twenty
dollars would not pay all of Janet's hospital and doctor
bills. It was not nearly enough. But—added to the money
that Mr. Mac would get from the sale of Prince and
Dreamdust—then might it not be enough? Might it not
make the difference between hope and despair for the
Macklins?

Dinny washed her face and changed her shirt. Then,

her chin high and her shoulders straight, she made a visit to the bank, and from there started back to the Lazy H.

At first, Mr. Mac refused. "Absolutely not!" he protested. "Good grief, girl, isn't it bad enough that you have to lose Dreamdust? I know you want to help, and I am grateful to you for it. But I will not accept that money!"

Dinny had said it before and now she repeated it. "Please, Mr. Mac. I want to do it. I—I need to. Please!"

He looked at her closely, and all at once his eyes clouded, so that for a moment Dinny was afraid that there were tears in them. "Dinny, dear." Mr. Mac's voice was very gentle now. "Do you still blame yourself for Jan's accident?"

Dinny couldn't answer, but she managed to nod.

"Oh, honey, you mustn't! It was not your fault. It was nobody's fault. Listen to me, Dinny. Will it make you feel any better if I accept that money of yours?"

Again she nodded. Mr. Mac put his arm around her. "Then I will accept. But only as a loan to the Lazy H. And—and thank you, Dinny. This means a great deal to me. To all of us."

A few moments later, for the second time that day Dinny walked away from the Lazy H toward the bus. "I can't go back," she told herself. "I can't go back to the

Lazy H any more. Not with Mike feeling the way he does about me. And not with Dreamdust gone."

This time she could not hold the tears back. "I have lost everything," she thought. "Dreamdust. My friendship with Mike. Being part of a family again. I have lost everything that matters most to me."

CHAPTER 11

"Fire, Fire!"

It was early in the evening, four days later. Dinny was sitting alone on the porch steps. "It certainly is lonesome and quiet around here," she thought. "I am used to all the activity at the Lazy H. Golly, how I miss riding! And how I do miss Dreamdust!"

Lissa Lambert had phoned yesterday to say that Prince and Dreamdust were at Cottonwood Hills, and everybody was very pleased with them. "One thing, Colonel Gill takes wonderful care of his horses," Dinny told herself, "so I don't have to worry about Dreamdust."

As Dinny raised her eyes, she saw a tall, trim figure turning in at the front walk. With a "Hi!" and a flip of her hand, Lissa Lambert joined Dinny on the steps.

"I came to see if you wouldn't like to go riding with

me at Cottonwood tomorrow. My treat, of course. Colonel Gill promised he wouldn't send Dreamdust out with anyone else if we get there before ten."

Dinny thought it over a moment, then shook her head slowly. "Lissa, thanks a lot, but—well, I can't let you pay for my riding, and I can't afford to ride at Cottonwood myself except maybe once in a great while. The way I see it, that would be worse than not riding Dreamdust at all. If I don't see her, I'll forget her pretty soon."

Dinny knew that was a lie, and so did Lissa. Silence settled down. Searching around for some way to break it, Dinny was about to remark that school would soon be starting again when a car drew up in front of the house. Both girls recognized it at once—the Macklins' old station wagon. They recognized the driver, too.

"There's Mike," they said, almost in chorus, but in entirely different tones. Lissa's was delighted, Dinny's dismayed.

Mike got out. Seeing Lissa, his face broke into a smile. "Hi, Lissa! Where have you been keeping yourself? We've missed you at the Lazy H." Then, to Dinny, "Mom sent me. Jan keeps asking why you don't come to visit her at the hospital. Mom says you probably have no way to get there, so she told me to come and drive you out."

Dinny did want to see Janet, though she didn't much care for the idea of a long ride with Mike. On the other hand, when Mike turned to Lissa and asked, "Don't you want to ride along, Lissa?" Dinny didn't much care for that idea, either.

"Sure," Dinny said then, "I would love to see Jan. I'll get a sweater and be right with you." When she came out of the house, Mike and Lissa were already in the car which, of course, put Lissa next to Mike on the front seat. *Very* next, Dinny noted.

All the way out to the hospital, which was in the town beyond Carney's Landing, Mike and Lissa talked almost without stopping. When they reached the hospital, Mike said, "Lissa and I will wait, Dinny. Mom is there, and Jan is allowed only two visitors at a time."

In spite of her casts and bandages, Janet was fairly comfortable and happy. "The doctor says if I keep on the way I'm going, I will probably be ready for school when it opens," she told Dinny.

"Dinny, we miss you out at the Lazy H," Mrs. Mac said. "I don't mean because of all the work you did. We miss *you*, Dinny dear. At least, come to visit us!"

They chatted for half an hour or so. By the time she left, Dinny felt almost as if she were part of the Macklin family again, sharing their problems and pleasures. But when she joined Mike and Lissa, the warm feeling disappeared. "Those two," she thought sadly, as Mike headed for Springfield, "hardly noticed I had come back!"

Dinny tried to keep her attention away from the laughter, the bright conversation going on beside her by making a game of picking out familiar things along the road. The little stand that sold such delicious ice cream. The farm market where they had such good watermelons. The turn-off to the Lazy H. But a thought kept coming back. *Mike still blames me.*

"Oh, stop it," Dinny told herself. "Think!" Right over there was the house with the beautiful row of poplar trees in front. Up ahead, around that curve, the entrance to Cottonwood Hills. Next . . .

"What's that red glow in the sky?"

"Where?" Mike asked. And then, to answer himself, "Golly, it looks like a fire. It looks—yes, it looks as if it might be right near Cottonwood Hills!"

He stepped on the gas. The nearer they came to the long curve, the bigger and brighter grew that red patch in the sky. Dinny felt her heart begin to pound, her breath come faster, and heard, from Lissa, a little moan of fright. As they swept around the curve, Mike cried, "It *is* Cottonwood! Look—the stable is on fire!" Without stopping he turned in, started speeding up the long, winding drive that led to the stables.

Very clearly, like a lesson learned and never forgotten, Dinny remembered what she had read about stable fires. "In a fire, horses seem to go crazy. Even though the stable is burning all around them, they don't want to leave their own stalls, because those stalls represent security to them. You have to cover a horse's eyes before you can lead him out of a burning building. When you have him out he has to be tied tightly or he will break away and run right back to his stall, even though it means he will be burned to death. He doesn't know this."

"You girls use your sweaters to cover the horses' eyes," Mike directed. "Dip them in the watering trough." It didn't occur to him, apparently, to ask Dinny and Lissa if they could help or if they would. They *had* to help. He slammed the car to a halt and tumbled out, Dinny close on his heels.

As she ran across the stable yard, Dinny could see that the whole second story of the huge barn, where hay and feed were stored, was on fire, sending up clouds of smoke, shooting tongues of flame. The roofs of the two L-wings which housed most of the horses had begun to smoke and, Dinny knew, would catch fire any moment.

The whole place was a confusion of smoke, of voices, of running figures. Colonel Gill and the stable boys had already brought out some of the horses and tied them to a fence at a safe distance, where they neighed and stamped, rolling their eyes in a wild way. From inside the barn came the stamping of hoofs and the screams of the frightened animals.

Snatching her sweater from around her shoulders, Dinny dipped it in the trough near the door and, without stopping, ran into the barn. She slipped into the first stall she came to, dodging the flying hoofs, and wrapped

the sweater around the horse's eyes, knotting the sleeves.

"Come on, boy," she said, taking hold of his reins. She tried to make her voice calm and full of authority, the kind of voice a horse knows he must obey. The horse moved, backed free of the stall, let her lead him, on the run, to the fence.

From then on, Dinny repeated the operation over and over again, working in a mechanical sort of way.

There was no time to think. Besides, she sensed, it would be fatal to think about the danger, to let fear enter her mind. Better to dip the sweater, find a horse, bring him out, go back and do it again—and again and again. Pay no attention to the roaring of the fire. Breathe lightly so as not to choke on the heavy smoke.

The thought of Dreamdust touched her mind, but she pushed it away. There was no time to search for one special horse. Others would perish while she searched. Just take the first horse you see. Work. Keep going. Dodge the other hurrying figures that are working as you are working, getting horses out. Keep going, keep going!

At last, as Dinny tied a horse to the fence and started back to the stable yet another time, a hand grabbed her.

She turned smarting eyes up to Mike's black face.

"We can't go back!" he cried, and a second later she knew why. With a terrible roar, a blast of flame and a cloud of greasy black smoke that reached to the sky, the whole second floor of the barn caved in.

Dinny felt Mike's arm around her shoulders and she leaned against him. Too weary to move, to think, they stood silent, staring at the flaming ruin of the barn. Finally Mike asked, in a strange, hoarse voice, "Are you all right? Wait a minute. I'll be right back."

She watched him move slowly, through the smoke, down the line of horses to the other end of the fence. She could just make out a knot of figures there. She recognized Colonel Gill and the four stable boys. Who were the others? Strangers, probably. Men who had stopped to help, seeing the smoke and flame.

In a minute or two Mike was back, wearing a tired but satisfied smile. "Dinny, we did it—we did it! We got every single horse out. Not one loss!"

"That—that's wonderful." But something was troubling Dinny, something vague but frightening lay in the back of her mind. And then, with a sharp cry of dismay, she knew.

"Mike! Where's Lissa? What's happened to Lissa?"

CHAPTER 12

Everything That Matters

Dinny stirred, turned over on her back, and opened her eyes. At first she didn't know where she was. In bed—but what bed? Not her own, at home in her own room. She could see, by the bright sunlight outside, that it was morning—but what morning?

Little by little she pieced everything together. The fire. The mixture of sights and sounds and fears. But it had turned out all right. She remembered Mike telling her that all the horses had been saved. And what else? Oh, yes! Lissa! Dinny sat up.

"Where is Lissa?" she had asked and Mike, full of scorn, said, "Don't worry about her. She is perfectly safe. She never even got out of the car!"

Something had changed in Mike, Dinny realized. The

way he had said, "Don't worry about *her!*" told Dinny that now he saw Lissa with different eyes. Colder eyes. Knowing this, Dinny felt odd. In spite of everything, Lissa was her friend.

"You must not blame Lissa, Mike," she had said. "She probably stopped to think about it, and then she couldn't make herself go in. That's the difference—you didn't stop to think and neither did I. That wasn't so very bright of us, if you come right down to it!"

Mike had shaken his head, not convinced.

"Thinking isn't something to be blamed for!" Dinny had protested, still defending Lissa. "Anyway, it's like what you told me about Janet being afraid of horses. All people are not alike, and we have no right to get mad at the ones who happen to be different from ourselves!"

The thing that she remembered best about last night, Dinny discovered then, was the look in Mike's eyes when he answered, "All right. You win. I won't blame Lissa. But I am not going to hang any medals on her, either."

Mike had said all this in a rather rough voice, almost as if he were trying to hide what he really meant. Then, meeting Dinny's eyes, he had said, "You were great, Dinny. Just great, that's all!"

"Mike does not blame me any more!" The words sang a song in Dinny's mind as she got out of bed. "Why— why, Mike is proud he knows me!"

She tried to piece together the rest of last night as she dressed. But she could not remember it all. One moment, for instance, she had been standing at the fence at Cottonwood Hills and the next she had been in the kitchen of the Lazy H, with Mrs. Mac offering her hot cocoa and making a fuss over her. But how she got between the two places was a complete blank. The very last thing she remembered was Mrs. Mac's saying, "You go on up and take a shower and hop into Janet's bed. Scoot! I will call your father and tell him where you are."

From downstairs floated up delicious smells of frying bacon and hot rolls. She was, Dinny realized, very hungry. Hurrying into the rest of her clothes, she took the stairs two at a time and burst into the kitchen.

Mrs. Mac, taking a pan of rolls from the oven, asked in an anxious voice, "How are you, honey?"

Before Dinny could answer, Mr. Mac did it for her. "She's fine. Didn't you hear her coming down those stairs? All I can say is, it's great to be young. If I had gone through what Dinny and Mike went through last night, I would be in bed for a week!"

But it was the way Mike greeted her that pleased Dinny most. "Hi!" he said. "It's about time you got up— I'm starving to death, but Mom wouldn't let us eat without you." It wasn't the words, but the tone of his voice—warm and friendly. Warmer and more friendly than ever before.

"Sit down," Mike went on, pulling out a chair at the big, round table. "You have missed a lot. Just wait till Dad fills you in on what happened after you went to bed last night. This is the best ever!"

"Don't start till I get the food on," Mrs. Mac protested. "I want to hear it all over again. I could hear it twenty times and it would sound better each time!"

"Whatever it is," Dinny thought as she helped Mrs. Mac pour orange juice, dish up bacon and eggs, "it must be pretty wonderful. I have never seen the Macs so excited and happy before!"

When they were all seated and served, Mr. Mac began his story. "Well, as soon as you kids turned up and told me what had happened at Cottonwood, naturally I went right over to see if there was anything I could do to help. Handling a lot of frightened horses is not an easy thing to do, you know." He stopped, laughing. "What do I mean, *you know?* If anybody knows, Dinny, you do!"

"Boy, is Colonel Gill ever impressed with you, Dinny," Mike put in. "He thinks Diane Stoner is just about the greatest invention since the wheel. So does everybody." He grinned, his face suddenly flaming. "Me, too!"

Dinny flashed him a quick smile, her heart singing. "Tell me the rest," she urged Mr. Mac.

"By the time I got to Cottonwood, Dr. Hansen, the animal doctor, was there looking over the horses. Aside from some skin scratches, a few small burns from falling sparks, and one pulled muscle, there wasn't an injury among all those horses. The colonel's insurance completely covers building the barn and stables again, so he has no worries there. The big thing troubling him was what to do with his horses till the new barns could be built."

Mr. Mac paused for a moment. "Colonel Gill was telling me this, when all at once he was struck with an idea. 'Say, Macklin,' he said, 'you have a lot of extra room over at the Lazy H. Your stall house is not more than half full and every stall in the barn is empty.' And then he made me an offer."

Dinny saw the smiles on the faces of all the Macklins. "Don't keep me waiting, Mr. Mac!" she said. "What offer did Colonel Gill make?"

"Well, it boils down to this—we are going to house the Cottonwood Hills horses here at the Lazy H until the new barns are ready. Of course the colonel will supply his own feed and send over one of his stable boys to help take care of the horses. And, of course, all the Cottonwood Hills riders will be sent over here, and the riding fees will be divided between Cottonwood Hills and the Lazy H. Realize what that means? Cottonwood's fees in one day are twice what the Lazy H takes in for a couple of weeks! Dinny, the Lazy H is saved!"

Dinny could only look from one to another, her eyes dancing. Finally she found the breath to say, "It's wonderful—oh, golly, it's just wonderful!"

"Dad forgot one other thing," Mike added. "The colonel will pay me as long as the horses are here. Regular guide's salary. So we are all set. More than all set, we are really rolling!"

He hesitated. "Well, except for one thing I want to say, Dinny—and I want to say it in front of Mom and Dad. I'm sorry I was so mean to you about Jan's accident. It *wasn't* your fault. It was as much my fault, because I encouraged Jan to ride Comanche, too. But as Dad said, it wasn't anybody's fault. It was an accident." He sighed with relief. "Well, that's off my chest! You finished, Din? Let's take a look at the new horses."

Dinny raised her eyebrows. "New horses? You mean the colonel's horses? They're already *here?*"

Mike laughed. "Sure. We moved them all last night. Some we rode over, and Colonel Gill's two big horse vans went back and forth half the night."

She could hardly believe it. "You mean all that went on, and I didn't even notice?" Dinny demanded.

"Girl, when you sleep you really put your heart and soul in your work!" Mike said. "Come on, let's go out!"

In the barn, Mike and Dinny inspected the long rows of sleek, handsome horses. Dinny saw Prince at once, but after looking carefully she turned anxious eyes to Mike. "Where is Dreamdust? She *is* all right, isn't she? Mike—"

"Dreamy's all right," he assured her. "I put her in her old stall, with our horses. Thought she might feel more at home there. Why don't you go in and—" But then he stopped. Dinny had already gone.

Sure enough, there was Dreamdust back home in her own stall. As Dinny's hurrying steps sounded down the runway, the little horse pricked up her ears and neighed in delight. With a cry of joy, Dinny slipped into the stall beside her, putting one arm around her neck. "Oh, Dreamy—I'm so glad to see you! I'm so glad you're safe!"

Dreamdust turned to nibble gently at the sleeve of Dinny's shirt. *I'm every bit as glad to see you,* she seemed to be saying. *I missed you, Dinny!*

"Oh, and I missed you, too," Dinny told her. "Maybe in a little while we will go for a ride, shall we? Up along the ridge?" And then she remembered. "If it's all right with Colonel Gill, that is," Dinny added, some of the pleasure gone from her voice. At Cottonwood Hills or back here at the Lazy H, Dreamdust was still the colonel's horse. There was no way to get around that.

"How about some breakfast?" Dinny asked the mare. "Had your oats yet?" Looking in the feed box, she found it empty. "If you did, you certainly licked the platter clean. Let's just take it for granted you haven't been fed. I'll be right back."

Dinny went down the runway to the big feed bins at the end and started back with a measure of oats. As she came near Dreamdust's stall, she saw that they had company. Colonel Gill was there, waiting for her.

"Good morning," he said, in a sharp, military voice. "I am glad to see you up and about. I was afraid you might be worn out, after last night."

"I'm fine, thank you," Dinny told him.

The colonel smiled at her. "You are better than fine, Dinny. You are the finest. That's what I came here for—to thank you, in person, for what you did last night. You were very brave."

"I wasn't really so brave," Dinny answered honestly. "It was—oh, I knew what would happen to the horses if they weren't taken out, and—well, I love horses so, I couldn't stand that! I *had* to help!"

The colonel turned to give Dreamdust's side a pat. "Handsome little mare you have there."

"Isn't she, though?" Then Dinny hesitated. "What—?"

Colonel Gill's eyes were twinkling. "Yes, you heard me right. Dreamdust *is* yours. I would be honored if you would accept her as a thank you for your help last night."

"Oh!" Dinny cried with joy. Then, the happy smile left her face. "But I—I can't accept her, Colonel Gill. Dreamdust is much too valuable!"

The colonel shook his head. "My dear, I *want* to give you Dreamdust. The fact that you saved me many times her value in blooded stock last night does not enter into it. You and Dreamdust belong together. I shall be very much hurt if you do not accept. Will you, under those circumstances?"

"Under those circumstances," Dinny said, delight bubbling in her voice again, "I can't very well say no. And oh—oh, thank you, Colonel Gill. Thank you so very much!"

"It is my pleasure," he said. With a nod that was almost a bow, he turned and walked out of the stable, still smiling to himself.

Dinny stayed with Dreamdust a while longer, trying to get used to the wonderful idea of owning her. But at last she said, "I can't neglect the other horses, you know. I will see that everyone's fed, and then we'll go for a ride, Dreamy. In a way, our first ride!" Still full of pleasure, but not quite able to believe her good fortune, Dinny began to feed the other horses.

After a little, Mike came in. "Everything all right in—hey, Dinny, what's up? You look sort of floaty."

"I am. I'm floating at least ten feet off the ground. Colonel Gill gave me Dreamdust. She's all mine!"

Mike grinned at her. "That's what he said he was going to do last night. Things are looking up all around, aren't they? But it's not going to be easy. We are all going to have to work like crazy around here. That means you too—if you will, Dinny. What do you say? Want to come back to being the lowest paid stable boy in the business?"

"Sure I do!"

"Well, hop to it then! We will finish feeding these horses and then I can get down some straw to bed them."

For a while they worked in silence. Dinny still had that ten-feet-off-the-ground feeling, and each time she passed Dreamdust's stall she reached out to touch her, just to make sure the little mare was real—and really hers!

"Wait till I tell Dad," she thought. Then she stopped, surprised. "Why, it's true! I'm not one bit worried about telling Dad, because now—well, now we see eye to eye. And isn't it wonderful?"

After the last horse on her side of the runway was fed, Dinny slipped back into Dreamdust's stall for a moment. "It's been such a wonderful summer," she whispered in the mare's ear.

She looked down the runway to where Mike was feeding the last horse on his side. "Well, most everything turned out right, at least."

"Ready?" Mike asked, coming up the runway. He climbed quickly up the ladder to the loft and, a moment later, appeared at the opening over Dinny's head. He began to send down straw, which Dinny in turn distributed among the stalls. They worked silently for a while. Then Mike called down through the opening. "Hey, Din, you know what?"

"No, what?"

"Turns out I'm not going back to Locust Valley for my senior year, after all. I can't leave Dad with all this extra work. And there will be plenty. So it looks as if I will have to go out for the Springfield High football team."

"Do you mind very much, Mike? About not going back, I mean?"

He shook his head. "Funny, but I don't. This place is beginning to seem like home to me. To tell the truth, I'm sort of glad. And it won't be too tough, starting out at Springfield High. You can show me the ropes, too, same as Janet. Right?"

140

"Right!" Dinny answered. Then she remembered. "Mike, you know Lissa goes to Springfield High, too." Now that everything was so right, so perfect, she could not stand the thought of a Mike-and-Lissa feud at school.

Mike grinned down at her through a cloud of straw dust. "So what? Listen, don't worry. Perhaps Lissa isn't my very favorite person. She never will be, after the way she acted! But . . . well, as you said, we can't all be alike."

Dinny sighed with relief. "I'm glad you feel that way. It spoils everything when people bear grudges."

"Why, I even took Lissa home last night," Mike continued, "though right then if I'd never laid eyes on her again it would have been too soon. Polite to the end, that's Mike Macklin for you. So don't give it another thought." He picked up his pitchfork. "Well, don't just stand there, girl. We have a lot of work to do. Let's get moving!"

"No, *sir!*" Dinny grinned back at him. "Yes, *sir!*" She grabbed her hay fork and began again to distribute hay to the stalls. As she worked, her mind was a winding stream of bright, shining thoughts. Mike was going to Springfield High. Dreamdust was hers. She was part of the Lazy H family again. She and her father were much more a real family than ever before. Yes, everything— every single thing that mattered—was hers again. All the important things that, less than a week ago, she had been certain were lost to her forever.

"Hey, what's with you?" Mike called down. "You look like a cat with feathers on its whiskers. You hatching some wild scheme?"

Dinny shook her head. "No. Just trying to remember something. It's not important."

It was important. Terribly important. But she couldn't very well tell Mike, could she, that what she was trying to remember was whether she had ever been this happy, or even nearly this happy, before in her whole life?